AFTER THE BLUE

AFTER THE BLUE

Russel Like

BRUNSWICK GALAXY PRESS

Brunswick Galaxy Press
P O Box 4213
Highland Park, NJ 08904
USA
e-mail: Farnstarfl@aol.com

Publisher's Cataloging-in-Publication
(Provided by Quality Books, Inc.)

Like, Russel C.
     After the blue / by Russel C. Like. -- 1st ed.
     p. cm.
     Preassigned LCCN: 97-97156
     ISBN: 0-9661039-0-4

     1. Life on other planets--Fiction. 2. Science fiction,
American. I. Title.

PS3562.I45465A48 1998   813'.54
                             QBI97-41387

Dedicated to my family

AFTER THE BLUE

Prologue

During the opening years of the twenty-first century, the human race got a definitive answer to one of its most burning questions—whether or not there was intelligent life elsewhere in the universe. The extraterrestrials who detected human radio signals and came to visit Earth were merely curious. Although they had long ago mastered the secrets of space travel, they had never before encountered another sentient race. Their visit to Earth was purely peaceful.

Yet within weeks of their visit, human societies across the planet had collapsed and well over ninety-nine percent of the human race was dead. It was as if human civilization were Humpty Dumpty and the extraterrestrials were the foolish and clumsy children who had accidentally pushed him off his wall.

So remorseful were the extraterrestrials at having ruined the only other civilization they had ever found that they began to rummage through the considerable quantity of human artifacts left on Earth in the hope that they might learn something about what it was that they had ruined. And as their scientists and sociologists pored over these artifacts, and began to piece together an idea of what the civilization they had destroyed had been like, they began to develop an appreciation for it. This led to the conclusion among them that all societies had a beauty, an intrinsic worth, of their own, and their regret at the destruction of human civilization grew even more profound.

The extraterrestrials numbered in the many trillions and controlled thousands of planets. They possessed vast, nearly inexhaustible resources, and their industries were extraordinarily productive. But this efficiency had a downside—the extraterrestrials were burdened with a veritable army of unemployed. And as their leaders reviewed the reports coming in from Earth, an intriguing thought occurred to them, an idea that could both alleviate their unemployment problem and serve an aesthetic purpose. The plan was made possible by the fact that, here and there, a few humans had managed to survive on Earth, and it was based on this concept: that it might be possible to put Humpty Dumpty back together again.

However, to the extraterrestrials, human society was, after all, alien, and this particular Humpty Dumpty was reassembled with a scrambled yolk.

Chapter 1

Sheila thought the Gruumsbaggian looked rather comical in his McDonald's uniform, with his four arms and red bulbous nose. The fact that he was stooping over so his head would not scrape the ceiling only added to the silliness of his appearance. She did her best to conceal her thoughts, though, because she generally liked Gruumsbaggians, even if she was beginning to suspect they weren't telling her everything. Besides, she wanted to do a good job. She tore open a bag of frozen french fries and poured them into the deep fryer. Then she sat down and waited.

"No, no, no," shouted the Gruumsbaggian, waving all his arms at her and stomping across the room. "That's not the way you do it at all! Look, let me show you again." He fished the discarded freezer bag out of the garbage receptacle and dumped the fries back inside. "First, we heat the oil," he said.

If Sheila had ever seen *Sesame Street*, she might have thought the Gruumsbaggian, whose name was hard to pronounce in English and whom she had therefore been told to call Fred, resembled nothing so much as a large and particularly officious muppet.

11

But she had never seen *Sesame Street,* or *The Muppet Show*, or *Gilligan's Island*, or *The Tonight Show*, or *Dallas*, or, for that matter, many television shows or movies at all. The only programs or films she had seen were those few which the Gruumsbaggians had found copies of on Earth and deemed appropriate for children's viewing. These included, among other things, twelve episodes of the *Flying Nun*, thirty-seven episodes of the cat-and-mouse cartoon *Tom and Jerry*, and the movie *Godzilla versus the Smog Monster.* For Sheila had been bred and raised on Gruums-Baag under the care and tutelage of Gruumsbaggians, and she had only recently, at the age of seventeen, been brought to Earth to work at McDonald's.

Sheila had been told by the Gruumsbaggians that she was being brought to Earth. But she was having a hard time believing that, since the Gruumsbaggians had also told her Earth was a place where millions upon millions of other humans lived, and almost no Gruumsbaggians. But so far she had seen a lot more Gruumsbaggians than humans. In fact she had not seen a single other human being since leaving Gruums-Baag. She spent a lot of time wondering why the Gruumsbaggians had lied to her, because obviously, they had either lied about this being earth, or they had lied about what Earth was like. She couldn't remember them ever lying to her before, although she was beginning to realize that she had never really had any way of determining whether they were telling the truth about most of the things they told her.

"Boy, it's hot in here," Fred said, fanning his yellow face with his small red cap. "You keep cooking and cleaning, okay? I'm going into the little room to cool off for a while." He mopped his banana-yellow brow with the backside of his upper left hand in what he thought to be a gesture a manager in a hot kitchen might make, although, like most Gruumsbaggians, he did not sweat.

"Okay," Sheila said. "I'll just put these chicken nuggets up in a minute, and then I'll get right on to cleaning the grill." She was still confused and a little uneasy, but she had not yet figured out what to do next.

Fred stepped into the little room, off in a corner, and stretched himself out to his full height of seven feet, four inches. The "little" room was not really so little, at least in terms of height, as it had been designed to comfortably accommodate even the largest Gruumsbaggian, and Fred was of average Gruumsbaggian height. He was also of average Gruumsbaggian appearance. He had the normal complement of four arms and two legs, and the typical vaguely humanoid Gruumsbaggian body shape and facial features. He had the shiny banana-yellow complexion universal among his race, and he had a perfectly ordinary Gruumsbaggian nose, which looked exactly as if someone had taken a smooth, five-inch long potato, covered it with bright red felt, and glued it vertically between and just beneath his big round orange eyes. He had the generic angular Gruumsbaggian face, and his head was crowned by the typical three-inch long bluish fur, standing straight up, which almost all Gruumsbaggians had. Unlike most Gruumsbaggians, he had only twelve pancreases, but this did not affect his appearance.

Not only was Fred an average Gruumsbaggian in nearly every physical respect. He also possessed an unrelentingly average Gruumsbaggian intelligence. He was not one of that handful of Gruumsbaggians who had given his race the secret of space travel, or the keys to an understanding of molecular biology, or the necessary tools to achieve dominion over ten thousand worlds. He was one of the countless ordinary Gruumsbaggians who pumped the Gruumsbaggian equivalent of gas, or worked on factory assembly lines, or labored in the fields and mines. He was one of the trillions who carried out the instructions of the handful at the top, and this was the real reason he had sequestered himself in the little room that functioned as both manager's office and all-purpose Gruumsbaggian lounge. For this room contained a variety of electronic equipment, and he needed help. He had actually forgotten, in his role as McDonald's manager, what he was supposed to do next. They had waxed the floors, and cleaned the tables, and made at least perfunctory preparations for every item of food. The lawn outside had been mowed, the shrubbery trimmed, and the hamburger wrappers and french-fry containers made ready. But now what? Fred plucked a videocassette from the shelf, inserted it into the machine, and stretched himself out on a long low couch to watch.

The videotape was scratchy and full of static, and snow seemed to fly diagonally across the screen. Occasionally the entire picture would float upwards, and a duplicate picture would rise to replace it from the bottom of the screen. The videotape, which had been salvaged from the wreckage of human civilization, represented a link between Old Earth and the present. It was a ten-minute instructional show compiled from tapes produced by the McDonald's Corporation when there had still been a McDonald's Corporation. The tape had been restored, through the prowess of Gruumsbaggian technology, to its current barely usable condition, along with several thousand other videotapes, audio cassettes, microfilms, and compact disks.

After The Blue

The videotape first showed smiling humans in McDonald's uniforms arriving at the restaurant against the backdrop of a rising sun. They all greeted one another, although Fred could not discern what they were saying because of the static, and then they promptly got to work. Some of them began preparing food. One took a mop and began vigorously washing the floor, swooping in and out among the tables and chairs. Another tended to the napkin dispensers, condiment racks, and garbage receptacles. Still others took up positions behind the cash registers, and one of them, a woman who was wearing a slightly different-looking uniform, hovered from group to group, occasionally darting in and out of the little room in the video McDonald's. Finally everyone ceased their activities, except for one person who unbolted the door. Then they all seemed to wait, doing next to nothing, until a woman, not wearing a McDonald's uniform, came through the unbolted door with a small child grasping either hand and headed for the cash registers.

Fred beat on his chest with all four hands and howled in the typical Gruumsbaggian gesture for 'Eureka' or 'boy-am-I-stupid-the-answer-was-right-there-all-the-time.' Customers! That was what they were supposed to do next. They were supposed to wait for customers. Then, when customers came in, they would place orders, and Sheila and Fred would give them food in exchange for currency. He would have to remember this.

He rushed out of the little room in such a hurry that he nearly forgot to stoop and almost banged his head on the low overhanging ceiling. "Sheila!" he called in his flat, bass voice, which, like the voices of most Gruumsbaggians, sounded similar to human voices, if just a little lower in pitch.

"Yes?"

"Get behind the cash register. We need to be ready for our customers." Fred wondered how, exactly, customers would be lured to the store. The debriefers had not been particularly clear about that, and he wasn't sure if the little room contained the proper videotapes. He would have to find out.

Fred knew that if he could just get the business going, then Sheila, if she did a good job, could eventually get promoted to manage a McDonald's of her own. From there, perhaps, she might move on to the Board of Directors, and perhaps, someday, to Chief Executive Officer herself. If she became Chief Executive Officer of McDonald's, Fred knew she would have to wear big red floppy shoes, a curly red wig, sleeveless yellow overalls, red-and-white striped pants, paint her face snow-white, and go by the first name 'Ronald,' but this seemed like a small price to pay for a position which provided such responsibility, and such respect from other humans. That was, the Gruumsbaggians had learned, the way the humans had run McDonald's in the past. Currently the 'Ronald' position was held by a Gruumsbaggian, of course, and a large office had been constructed for him in New York City.

There were not even any human managers of individual McDonald's, not yet at any rate. The Gruumsbaggians believed that the only way the humans would learn how to live properly—that was, the way they had lived before the Gruumsbaggians' first visit to Earth—was by following the examples.of others. Therefore the Grumsbaggians were requiring the human employees of McDonald's to start out as restaurant staff, and the positions of the entire Board of Directors, from the 'Ronald' position, to the one who had to wear the furry blue suit and drink a lot of milk shakes, to the one who spoke unintelligibly and stole hamburgers, were currently filled by Gruumsbaggians. The humans would watch and learn.

This re-creation of the former state of affairs on Earth had been pieced together in painstaking detail by Gruumsbaggian research teams over the course of decades. It had never occurred to Fred to question the accuracy of their historical research. He knew his job, and he thought he did it well enough. He was supposed to train Sheila, and the other humans sent to him by headquarters, to run the McDonald's properly. He was playing a crucial role in returning humans to their natural place in the cosmos, the place they had occupied until that Gruumsbaggian scouting team made such a fateful mistake a century earlier.

Fred rushed back to the little room and began to rifle through the tapes and documents inside. Surely there would be *something* about how to attract customers.

Sheila waited silently at the cash register. She wondered why the Gruumsbaggians behaved so strangely sometimes. It was becoming more and more apparent to her that Gruumsbaggians were very different from humans. But they were usually polite, and always seemed to treat her and the other young humans kindly. That made it all the more vexing that they had lied to her. When they had told her she would be leaving Gruums-Baag, all they had said was "We're taking you and your unit, and a lot of other humans, to Earth now," and she had gone willingly enough. It sounded like a great adventure. The thought of disobeying them hadn't even crossed her mind. After all, the Gruumsbaggians were the only parents she had ever known.

She missed the other humans from her unit. They had been put on different transports, but she had been assured that she would see them soon enough. Now, though, she was beginning to doubt that. She wondered if the Gruumsbaggians would have been more candid with her if she had behaved differently in the past. She wondered what she could possibly have done to earn their mistrust, but could think of nothing. She had always been very attentive in the classes the Gruumsbaggians required her to attend. They had taught her to read, of course, and to do math.

And then there were the history lessons. She had never learned any history about Gruumsbaggians. The history was always about Earth. 'Earth,' as the Gruumsbaggians described it, had been a place simply teeming with humans. There was a long human history on Earth, the Gruumsbaggians had taught them. On Earth, humans had achieved great triumphs, and been involved in wars and revolutions, and generally done all manner of things. On Earth, humans actually taught school; they hadn't just been students like they were on Gruums-Baag. On Earth, humans ran all sorts of operations—things called 'restaurants,' and 'malls,' and other 'businesses.' But the history lessons always seemed to end when the Gruumsbaggian instructors got to the part about the wars in places they called the 'Old Soviet Union' and 'Yugoslavia.' It was unclear to Sheila how long ago any of these wars had occurred, or what was happening on Earth now. The Gruumsbaggians would never give the slightest details, and when pressed by their students about visiting Earth, the Grumsbaggians had always said things like 'Oh, it's the off season,' or 'the mosquitoes are bad right now,' or 'the air fares are very high this time of year.' But one day that had changed. The transports had brought them to this place and now the

Gruumsbaggians claimed she was actually *on* Earth. Whenever she asked him about it, which was more and more frequently as she grew more and more uneasy, Fred always insisted that "of course they were on Earth." Sheila wondered, if that were true, why it wasn't more exciting.

She looked around at the vacant tables and chairs, the antiseptic floor and walls of the McDonalds. It certainly didn't look like 'Earth' to her. She wondered, for the umpteenth time since being brought there, why the Gruumsbaggians were not telling her everything.

Fred came rushing out of the little room again, in such haste that this time he did bang his head against the ceiling. He was not paying attention because he had just discovered that the attraction of customers required notices called 'advertisements' in newspapers, and on television, and on billboards along highways, and he had no idea whether plans had even been made to establish some of those things on Earth yet. In fact, he had no idea the restoration of human civilization would be so complicated. He hoped the planners of the whole operation back on Gruums-Baag had thought of all of these things. He was wondering how he would go about creating advertisements when Sheila addressed him with a question. "Fred," she said, and if Fred had been a more astute student of human facial expressions and intonation he would have marveled at the uncharacteristically serious, purposeful way in which she spoke, "why did you and the other Gruumsbaggians bring me and the other humans here?"

Fred paused. She had asked where they were before, and he had answered willingly, but this question was a bit different. It seemed to call for a more dramatic response. "Come outside with me here, Sheila," he said, patting her affectionately on the back with his lower left hand. "Come with me and I'll show you."

Leaving the mingled aroma of french fries and ammonia behind, they walked out the door and into the brilliant sunlight and cool breezes of an early spring afternoon. They walked across the manicured lawn, past luxuriant shrubs and the empty, desolate parking lot. Fred ignored the towering oaks which pushed up against the McDonald's on every side but the front, and he ignored the new, untraveled road which the Gruumsbaggians had just finished building and which connected to the parking lot. Instead, he led Sheila directly to the adjoining golden arches which loomed over the front lawn like a pair of behemoth upright horseshoes. He pointed to them, again placing his lower left hand against Sheila's back in a gesture of support and affection. "Sheila," he began—and if he had been human his voice would have been choked with sentiment—"Sheila, we have brought you home. To Earth."

Sheila looked at the arches. She looked at the colossal column-like things—'trees,' she knew they were called, from the lecture the Gruumsbaggians had given her on Earth botany. She peered up and down the smooth shiny road, so new it was faintly redolent of tar. She scanned the sky. She shut her eyes and listened intently for sounds of human life, but all she heard was the discordant cacophony of insects and the melodious chirping of thousands of birds. "But...this can't be Earth!" she said, shaking her head. "I don't care if there *are* trees here. It just can't. There are no people!"

Fred blinked his big orange eyes in the sunlight. He looked at the trees and the road and the restaurant. She was right. There weren't any humans around at all. He wondered if he should try to explain and then thought better of it.

***

There were in fact humans on Earth who had not been brought by the Gruumsbaggians. They were not very numerous, but they were not very far away. They actually had houses, and schools where human teachers taught human students, and farms, and factories where things were made. They lived and struggled and loved and labored and died just like Earth humans always have. But it would be a while before Sheila would encounter any of them.

Chapter 2

About twenty miles to the south of Fred and Sheila and their McDonald's, two young men were watching in a combination of horror and astonishment as a horde of Gruumsbaggians carted all sorts of things into a mall. The two young men were hiding behind a cluster of trees, where they felt there was a good chance the Gruumsbaggians would not see them. They did not want to be seen by the aliens because they believed that Gruumsbaggians were thoroughly vile. They believed that Gruumsbaggians were far worse than any human villain—far worse than Adolph Hitler, or Joseph Stalin, or Attila the Hun, for example. Like all of their family and friends, the two young men considered these archetypes of human evil to be mere thugs, petty criminals, when compared to the Gruumsbaggians.

Astonishment was mixed with the young men's horror because Gruumsbaggians were the last things they had expected to see at the mall. Before they had seen the Gruumsbaggians, the aliens had entered their thoughts and conversation only very indirectly. In fact the young men had been discussing, among other things, a decision about marriage that one of them would be receiving the next day.

The two young men had made their way to the mall by foot, in the pleasant chill of early spring, on a narrow dirt path which wound like a pale brown ribbon through miles of thick forest. The path had been hacked from the wilderness that had reclaimed land once dotted with the ranch houses and meticulously trimmed lawns of suburban New Jersey. The young men were dressed in crude trousers and shirts, and sweaters made of wool, and they both carried pistols. One was of average height, with light brown hair and plain features. The other one, who was a bit younger, was tall and thin, with a pale complexion, a large curved nose, and an unruly mop of reddish hair, and he had been unhappy even before they encountered the Gruumsbaggians.

"So anyway," the shorter, brown-haired one had said, as they set out on the path, "you're worried about what they might say tomorrow. You're worried they'll tell you it's a choice between Debra and Mary, or something like that."

The red-haired young man snorted. "That's the same as no choice at all. Would you want either of them? Okay, maybe that's a little harsh. I just don't think I'd be compatible with either one. I mean, we're so limited. It never used to be this way before the Blue. There used to be thousands of girls for each guy to choose from. I know you weren't happy when they told you, Jack. Tell me the truth. Is that why you're not married yet?"

"Yeah, I know, Henry. I'm not sure how compatible I'll be with any of my choices. But my parents weren't thrilled with each

23

other to begin with, and now they seem happy enough. So maybe it isn't that bad after all. And anyway, it's better than having a kid with two heads."

Of course Jack knew it was unlikely that any child would be born with two heads. He had simply been exaggerating. Still, he knew the geneticists were right when they insisted on determining who everyone in the community would be allowed to marry. In a community as small as theirs, where the people had been together for so long, they had to be extremely careful to avoid inbreeding. While two-headed babies were unlikely, babies with no thumbs, or with eyes that did not see, or with water where their brains should have been, were not unheard of.

"And," Henry added, "maybe you'll be lucky and a wanderer will turn up. Hey! Maybe I'll be lucky, too."

"Not likely! How long has it been? Twelve years? They must all be dead by now. I'll bet we never see another wanderer again."

***

While Jack and Henry were walking towards the mall, and while Fred was teaching Sheila how to prepare french fries, Gruumsbaggian laborers on Segment 4-J25 of the Earth Project were putting a few last touches on their appointed tasks at their work site in the area called Pennsylvania. After extensive trial runs, they had finally gotten all their flying brooms into working order. Now, whenever one of them lost control and came hurtling out of the sky to collapse in a heap on the forest floor or tangled in tree branches with bristles sticking out of his mouth, the accident was blamed on pilot error rather than mechanical failure. The Gruumsbaggians knew, from human books they had read and human movies they had seen, that humans had had flying brooms in the past. And while they had no problem manufacturing flying brooms—such a task was child's play for Gruumsbaggian science—they were having a very hard time learning how to fly them, especially when encumbered by the wrinkled black robes, pointed hats, and fake noses the humans had apparently worn when riding around on such brooms. The Gruumsbaggians marveled at the dexterity and balance of those humans—most of whom seemed to have been fragile elderly women—and the Gruumsbaggian were growing concerned that they would not be ready to teach young humans how to fly the brooms properly when their segment of the project was activated in two weeks.

Then the news came from Central Planning. Further research had revealed that even those humans who did fly around on brooms only did so once a year, at the end of the period the humans called October. The Gruumsbaggians on Segment 4-J25 breathed a collective sigh of relief. Now they would have more time to practice.

***

"I know what I'll do!" Henry said brightly as the two of them made their way along the path, their shoes leaving faint prints in the sandy soil. "Maybe I'll go off on my own. I'll become a wanderer myself, and I'll end up at some other town like Jamesburg, and then they'll *have* to let me marry whoever I want, because I won't be related to anyone. How does that sound?"

"Oh, just wonderful. First of all, you'll probably never *find* another town like Jamesburg. What did the Mayor say the other day? Something like 'we have every reason to believe that the six thousand of us here in Jamesburg represent the last outpost of humanity on the entire planet.' And second, the Blue was a long time ago, Henry, and you've heard about..."

"I know, I know. The wild dogs," Henry said, fingering his pistol. He sighed and took a deep breath of the fresh New Jersey spring air. "It was just a thought. I wish I'd been born before the Big Blue."

"You sure about that?" Jack asked. "Would you have wanted to spend all of your time in some stuffy little office?"

"But they didn't have to worry about wild dogs!"

"And we don't have to worry about pollution, or crime, or war, or poverty, or hunger, or racism, or a lot of other things."

"Well, you're the historian," Henry said. "If it made things so much better, than why is it officially called 'the catastrophe'?"

"Hey, I don't call it that. It's only some old people, like Ferdinand, who do. I'm not so sure it was a catastrophe at all. None of my friends or family died in it. As far as I'm concerned, it's just another historical event. And I've studied the way things used to be. I'm really not so sure that we aren't better off in a lot of ways."

Jack was almost certain he wouldn't have been happy in the world before the Big Blue. The thought of having to spend nearly all of his time in an office was repugnant to him, and he could hardly believe anyone had ever let themselves live that way. The only thing that ever really bothered Jack about his life was the same thing currently bothering Henry. But Jack realized there was nothing he could do to change things. He had resigned himself to the situation. He felt he could probably grow to be happy with Alice or Grace or Miriam, the girls the geneticists told him he could marry, even if he felt none of the instant burning love for any of them that he read about in books published before the Big Blue.

Still, that didn't mean Jack did not sympathize with Henry. Jack knew it was normal to be worried before the decision was made. In fact the decision amounted to a rite of passage for the people of the little community of Jamesburg. Circumstances and history had made it so. And sometimes Jack resented the fact that events preceding his birth had such a profound effect on the way he had to conduct his life. It seemed unfair to live under the legacy of the past, trapped by the present which that past had shaped for him. He had thought all of this through before, when he had received his own choices for marriage, but he still occasionally allowed himself to entertain notions of how things might have been. He would day-dream of a world much like his own, for example, but in which there were hundreds of thousands, maybe even millions, of humans. Or he would imagine a world in which genetics did not matter, or one in which three quarters of the eligible girls and women reasonably close to him in age were not his first, second, or third cousins. Sometimes he even tried to picture life in the world before the Big Blue, but without cars, or with advanced space travel, or without war. Jack liked to imagine. He would soon find out this was a good thing.

***

The Gruumsbaggian workers on Segment 12-OJ13 of the Earth Project had already been activated. They had been assigned to acculturate a shipment of young human children who had just arrived from Gruums-Baag, and they were teaching them how to behave on Earth. But they were having some slight problems. As they had been instructed, they were taking the children on at least one wild goose chase a day. The problem was not with the children, who were participating in the wild goose chases enthusiastically enough. The problem was with the geese. There were plenty of geese around, but whenever the Gruumsbaggians, their heavy yellow feet pounding the ground as they ran, got anywhere near the geese, the geese would inevitably take off in a chorus of squawks. The little children, who usually ran behind the Gruumsbaggians, seemed to be having fun; but the Gruumsbaggians were concerned. They wondered what kind of adults these children would become, if they were always frustrated in the pursuit of wild geese. The fact that they would have no idea of what to do with the geese, if they ever caught any, was the least of their worries.

But the Gruumsbaggians of Segment 12-OJ13 were not failing completely. They were having some success in teaching the human children how to crumble cookies, bounce balls, and drop toast on the ground so that it fell butter-side down.

***

As they walked along over the path, their feet crunching on twigs, or springing on soft piles of leaves, Jack remembered that Henry was doing him a favor. "Thanks again for coming with me, Henry," he said. "I really appreciate it."

Henry rubbed his hands together and drew his sweater closed, as they had come to another spot where the trees shaded the sun. "My pleasure. What are friends for?" he said, grinning. "What

28

else could I do, when Jamesburg's apprentice historian asks me to join him on an historical expedition?"

Jack smiled back. "Right," he said. "It would've been nice if we didn't have to walk, though."

Jack was grateful that Henry agreed to come along with him. The path was still not terribly well known, and the Mayor insisted anyone traveling on it take a companion for protection against the wild dogs. Of course it could not have been foreseen that they would encounter Gruumsbaggians. As far as the people of Jamesburg could tell, Gruumsbaggians had not been to Earth in over a century.

"So why, exactly, do you want to see this Mall, anyway?" Henry said. "What makes it any different than the Mall of Brunswick?" To Henry a Mall was a Mall.

"Oh, there are huge differences," Jack said. "The Mall of Brunswick has been used as an auto repair and storage shed for, I don't know how many years. It's just not authentic anymore. But, the Mall of Freehold, well, we might actually learn something about how things used to be." The people of Jamesburg had enough buildings closer to home and had left the Mall of Freehold, which was several miles away from their town, largely undisturbed.

As Jamesburg's apprentice historian, it was Jack's responsibility to be well-informed about the circumstances of every significant incident that had taken place in Jamesburg since the Blue, and to be reasonably well-informed about how things were prior to the Blue. He even knew a fair amount, as much as anyone still living could reasonably be expected to know, about the Big Blue itself. Jack had been apprentice historian ever since Jules, the former senior historian, had died two winters ago, leaving thirty-eight year old Harold and sixty-one year old Ferdinand as sole historical authorities in Jamesburg, and they, in accordance with the rules established by Rosenthal, had been obliged to train one of the youths in their area of expertise. So during those times when he was not helping to cut timber, or work the fields, or care for the livestock, or repair buildings, or otherwise participating in the physical maintenance of Jamesburg, he was expected to research the past and chronicle the present. The physical activities took him about fifteen hours each week. But even with the other responsibilities, he had plenty of time to enjoy the fresh, clean New Jersey air, to join in the daily softball and frisbee games that some of the men held whenever the weather permitted, or to spend time at the beach, lazily boating in canoes and rowboats. Like most of the people of Jamesburg, Jack did not live to work, but worked to live, to have enough clothes, and enough to eat and drink, a roof over his head, and electricity and heat.

***

All over the planet, Gruumsbaggian research teams continued their work. There was so much to learn, and even though the Earth Project had already begun, new data could always be accommodated. Some of the researchers had become particularly intrigued by the humans' complex transportation system. They had already figured out how cars and trucks and buses and trains and airplanes had gotten people from one place to another, but they were having a harder time with some of the other devices the humans had used. The Gruumsbaggians had noticed that, in spots, the humans had concentrated a strange assortment of machines to move themselves around. The Gruumsbaggians had dusted off the remnants of these machines and had gotten them working again. And, in an attempt to further their understanding, they tried riding around in these machines themselves. But even when they went around in circles on the backs of the plastic horses, or traveled through troughs filled with water while sitting on imitation fiberglass logs, or sat in little seats attached to the perimeters of rotating vertical disks, they made no headway. All of these things brought them right back where they had started. The Grumsbaggians were perplexed.

And it was even worse when they got to the machine where the seats spun around and around and around on a horizontal disk. That one made them throw up.

***

"So anyway," Jack said, as they drew closer to their destination, "this should be interesting. I've heard some remarkable things about the Mall of Freehold."

"Like what?" Henry asked. He did not share Jack's enthusiasm for history, but he wanted something to take his mind off of the news he would receive the next day, which he was sure would be bad, and off the cold, which was making his fingers numb.

"Well, for one thing, it's still almost entirely intact." Most of the structures built before the Blue had collapsed or burned, or at the very least, had gaping holes in their walls and ceilings. Those were the buildings the people of Jamesburg had chosen not to use, of course, and the buildings they did use had been patched with whatever materials happened to be handy, or had been constructed from logs and scraps of material cannibalized from old buildings. But Freehold had weathered the years a bit better. "I've heard some of the signs inside the building still exist and that there's actually still some merchandise left. I guess that would be where the birds living inside the mall haven't done too much damage." The Mall of Brunswick had been inhabited by pigeons, robins, and starlings for as long as anyone could remember, and no one had been able, or had bothered, to drive them out. "Just think, there could even be books! We might discover something really important."

A lot of books had been saved by Rosenthal and the other founders of Jamesburg just after the Big Blue, but much knowledge had still been lost. Jack allowed himself for a moment to entertain the thought that he might find the book that would explain how they could rebuild and operate something like the Internet, and a shiver ran up and down his spine.

"Do you think we'll be able to figure out how to build nuclear reactors again?" Henry asked, growing interested. He had always thought the concept of power sources which tended to spontaneously blow up to be rather fascinating.

"Um, I don't know," Jack said. He wasn't really sure how nuclear reactors worked anyway. "Why? Do you want that to be your specialization or something?" he asked.

"Just wondering. Wait! Did you hear that noise? Sounded a little like thunder."

"Yeah. Sort of early in the year for thunder, though. And I don't see any clouds."

In the distance, the path opened to bright sunlight. Beyond that, they caught a glimpse of the Mall of Freehold. It was enormous, much larger than the Mall of Brunswick, and Jack felt a reverential awe as its walls loomed over him. He had never seen such an imposing edifice. He wondered if it inspired any of the other people of Jamesburg when they saw it. He wondered if it could be used to help them appreciate history, if it could give them an understanding of Jamesburg before the Blue, to give them a feeling of where their community was coming from and where it might be going. He wondered if it might help give the people of Jamesburg a sense of historical perspective.

"You know what might be a good idea?" Jack said.

"What?" replied Henry, who was not very interested. He was still thinking about the idea of building nuclear power plants.

"We could hold some sort of historical festival at the Mall of Freehold. It could be like a holiday, and people who want to participate could act the roles of people who could have been found at the Mall before the Big Blue. We could have all the different types!" Jack thought about what the relevant texts said on the subject. "There would be the Mall Rat, and the Geek, and the Yuppie, and..." he said, growing more excited. He knew it would take some research. But he also knew that it was not without precedent. He knew people had done that sort of thing before, at historical places like Williamsburg, Virginia and Sturbridge, Massachusetts. And he would be able to use Jamesburg's library of books to help recreate the past. For a moment, the idea had him truly excited. It was invigorating to apply his imagination to a concrete project.

"Uh, well, I don't know, Jack," Henry said. "It's an interesting idea, but..."

"But what?"

Henry thought for a minute and realized the only fault he could find with the idea was that it wouldn't do a thing to change

33

the geneticists' decision about the girl he would be allowed to marry. It would not bring unrelated girls—preferably attractive ones with nice personalities between the ages of fifteen and twenty to whom he was completely unrelated—to Jamesburg. "Oh, I dunno. If it's a good idea, then why hasn't somebody thought about all this before?" he said.

This was the point at which they emerged from the path into the clearing and got the first indication that the Mall of Freehold was no longer a derelict pile of bricks and concrete. Beside it stood a huge machine, which was obviously the source of the thunder-like rumblings they had been hearing. Like the Mall, the machine was huge, but it was moving. It looked something like the one yellow bulldozer that Jamesburg had, but it was much bigger, and it was slate-gray. It had several arms and protrusions with which it was manipulating a section of the Mall's wall. Besides the rumbling, it emitted creaks and hisses and other noises which were so loud they were plainly audible to Jack and Henry even though they were hundreds of yards away. At first Jack thought what he perceived as the machine's movement might just be the way the sun was reflected off of the metal, but he soon realized, with deepening horror, that it was not. And the tall, yellow-skinned, blue-haired, four-armed figure motioning from atop the clanking, rotating machine could only be one thing.

"Oh my god," Jack murmured.

"Is that what I think it is?"

Jack nodded solemnly. "A Gruumsbaggian," he whispered, and pulled Henry back into the shadows of the trees. Of course Jack had never seen a live Gruumsbaggian, but most of the people of Jamesburg had at least a general idea of what they looked like, and

After The Blue

Jack, who knew the accounts of the Big Blue and the founding of Jamesburg by heart, had read descriptions of their appearance. At the sight of the Gruumsbaggian he felt his heart constrict. Hadn't the Gruumsbaggians already done enough to the human race? What could they be planning now? And how could a mere handful of humans ever hope to fight off the representatives of a galaxy-spanning empire?

***

For all his historical knowledge, neither Jack, nor any other citizen of Jamesburg, understood or even guessed that the consequences of the Gruumsbaggians' actions a century earlier had been a colossal mistake. It had never even occurred to them that a race of beings who had mastered space travel and advanced technology could make such a goof. As far as the people of Jamesburg were concerned, the Gruumsbaggians had acted out of spite and malice and cold calculation. They thought the Gruumsbaggians had just wanted to make sure humans would never challenge their dominion over the galaxy. But previously Jack had believed that the Gruumsbaggians had left Earth to the remnants of the human race in a tiny gesture of magnanimity. Now it was beginning to look like the Gruumsbaggians had returned to finish the job.

***

"We have to get closer," Jack said, crouching behind a bush. "We have to see what they're doing. We need to tell the council what's going on." He held up his pistol and gestured to Henry to follow him.

"Oh yeah, this is a good idea," Henry muttered. "The two of us with pistols and we're going to beat all the Gruumsbaggians." Suddenly he was no longer very concerned about the news he would be receiving the next day. He was more concerned about surviving *until* the next day. He was young and impetuous, and if he were alone he might have just run away.

They sat for awhile peering at the collosal machines and the Grumsbaggians who moved about, swinging their arms, the sun shining off their banana-yellow skin.

"Look," Jack whispered, "if they really want to kill us, I'm sure they'll do it no matter what we do. They didn't have much trouble a hundred years ago, so we might as well investigate."

Henry nodded. "Okay, fine. You're right. Let's go."

They began to pick their way through the edge of the woods to the jagged edge of the disintegrating pavement where the old parking lot began. The parking lot itself was now no more than large rocks and patches of asphalt with grass and weeds and an occasional small tree pushing up through the cracks. There was something like this situation at the Mall of Brunswick, though there a gravel road to and from the building had been kept in good repair. Unlike the Mall of Brunswick, though, the vegetation poking through the pavement near the Mall of Freehold had been cropped quite short.

***

In fact, a Gruumsbaggian with a lawn mower had gone over the weeds just a day or two earlier. This particular Gruumsbaggian, who had the misfortune to be allergic to pollen, had been sent to an infirmary in Earth orbit. There, Gruumsbaggian physicians were trying to control the swelling of his oblong red nose, which had ballooned to the size of a zucchini.

***

As Jack and Henry drew closer they could see there were more Gruumsbaggians on the ground around the large machine. They seemed to be operating a variety of small equipment: carts, wagons, and trucks. The large machine was clearly doing something to the wall of the Mall at a point which must have housed one of the department stores. Jack briefly wondered which one: Macy's, Sear's, K-Mart? The Gruumsbaggians seemed to be shouting noises to one another over the clamor of their machinery, and they did not appear to realize they were being watched, so Jack and Henry moved closer. They were able to get within thirty feet of one of the Gruumsbaggians without, they thought, alerting it of their presence.

Actually, the Gruumsbaggian did notice them, but didn't care. He had other things to worry about. He had been ordered to unload thirty-seven cartons of toothpaste, forty-four crates of grapefruit, nineteen cases of turtleneck sweaters, and fifteen live orangutans, among other things, into the Mall by the end of the day, and he was behind schedule.

This Gruumsbaggian was driving around in a little car pulling a flatbed cargo truck about fifteen feet in length. The flatbed was stacked to a height of six feet with identical copies of a shiny new book. No matter how much the cart swayed or turned, the books did not fall off.

"Books!" Jack exclaimed through a whisper. "New ones!" The only real books they ever saw were at least a hundred years old.

The Gruumsbaggian pulled the cart to a stop and stepped down to the cracked cement.

For a moment, Jack forgot his fear and pulled Henry forward, straining to read the title on the covers.

"What does it say?"Even Henry was interested. He had never seen a *new* book.

"I... I can almost make it out," Jack said. "The print's pretty large." They moved a few feet closer, remaining behind the vegetation, and peered at the shiny covers.

Jack read the title out loud. "Rediscovering Your True Self: How To Reduce Co-dependency, Restart The Fires Within, And Find the One to Spend the Rest of Your Life With," he read out loud.

Henry was staring at the books in open-mouthed awe. "Maybe I should get a copy of that," he said. "What else do they have here?"

Jack did not answer him for a moment. This book did not look like a weapon of destruction. He wondered if it could be something just as devastating, but perhaps more insidious. "Yeah. Let's see what else they have."

The Gruumsbaggians had a great many other things. They brought in one cart filled with goldfish swaying back and forth in little bowls, and another one brimming with cartons of "NoSmel, The Superlative Underarm Deodorant," and still another with copious quantities of frozen pizzas, and another with boxes which each had, on the side, a picture of a long-necked plastic duck dunking its head in a glass of water. There were many other objects, some of which neither

After The Blue

Jack nor Henry could even begin to identify. They fell back to the woods and watched for at least an hour. They thought one Gruumsbaggian noticed them, but the creature took no action and though they were trembling with fear, Jack and Henry stayed and continued to watch from the safety of the trees. Finally they decided they had seen enough to report back to the council, and, almost as puzzled as they were frightened, they began making their way back through the woods towards Jamesburg.

Chapter 3

That evening, at an emergency session of the council, Jack and Henry told of what they had seen. The mood in Council Hall on Railroad Avenue was grim. "So anyway," Jack said, "that's it. We saw them, and there were a lot of them. But I can't tell you that what they were doing looked dangerous."

The meeting room erupted into a chorus of angry, anguished voices.

"We're all doomed!" one person shouted. "They've come back to finish what they started a hundred years ago!"

"What can we do against them?" yelled another.

"They won't take me without a fight!"

"We have to leave Jamesburg and go someplace where they won't be able to find us!"

"Maybe they're not really Gruumsbaggians. Maybe Jack and Henry aren't telling the truth at all!" someone shouted from the back of the room.

The hubbub finally subsided to the rhythmic pounding of a heavy shoe on a wooden desk. It was Mayor Blanchard. "People!

After The Blue

People!" he yelled, putting his shoe back on once he had gotten everyone's attention. "Please quiet down. This is a very serious matter and we absolutely must have a rational discussion. Remember the pack of wild dogs that threatened us about ten years back? Remember how we were disciplined about it and how we managed to kill some of them and drive the rest off?" He added these details for the benefit of Jack, who was only twenty-one, and for Henry, who was eighteen, and who might not remember much about the routing of the dogs.

"Well, if we're not disciplined about this," the Mayor continued, "then we're in for a lot of trouble. One of you, I believe, mentioned something about not believing that the Gruumsbaggians have returned? I, for one, believe Jack and Henry. They've always been as responsible as any other boys their age. Now, please. One at a time."

Mayor Blanchard was a dark-haired, heavyset man in his mid-forties. He had a round face and a luxuriant mustache. If the people of Jamesburg had been familiar with twentieth-century television commercials, they might have said he resembled Beefsteak Charlie. He had been Mayor ever since being appointed at the age of thirty-two. Most people thought he did a pretty good job, even though he had been appointed by his father, who had been the previous Mayor.

***

In one of the retraining centers for the unemployed on Gruums-Baag, the instructor was preparing his pupils for their new jobs on Earth. "Now, every Saturday morning, just as the sun

41

comes up, you must jump out of your beds. You all remember what those are?"

"I don't remember," said one of the Gruumsbaggian pupils. "What are they again?"

"Where humans sleep."

"Right."

"So anyway, you jump out of your beds when the sun comes up, and then you put on your shorts and your T-shirts. And then what do you do? Does anyone remember? Anyone?" The instructor, just like instructors everywhere, was hopeful and encouraged when his students remembered things, and frustrated and disappointed when they didn't.

Not a single Gruumsbaggian raised a hand, right or left, upper or lower. "Okay, I'll tell you," the instructor finally said. "You mow the lawn."

Now one of the pupils raised a hand, the upper right, which, in a student-teacher relationship, signified only slight deference.

"Yes?" said the instructor.

"What does 'mow' mean again?"

The instructor buried his face in all four hands in the traditional Gruumsbaggian gesture of exasperation. Two more days, he told himself. Two more days until the last Earth training class full of unemployed Gruumsbaggians, who were often unemployed with good reason, would be over and all of his pupils would be shipped off the planet.

***

42

After The Blue

At Council Hall on Railroad Avenue in Jamesburg, Councilor Desmond Ghewen was telling the assemblage why the return of the Gruumsbaggians to Earth wasn't necessarily all that bad. It wasn't that Ghewen was stupid—quite the contrary. He had some very good reasons for providing the opinions that he did, even if he was, when you got right down to it, wrong. He was just pointing something out. "There is something no one has considered," he was saying. "Perhaps the Gruumsbaggians have changed. Yes, it's true that what they did a hundred years ago was certainly one of the most evil deeds ever perpetrated on this planet. But have not human societies changed? I don't know how many of you, historians excepted, have read the accounts of pre-catastrophe human history. Didn't the Evil Empire of the Soviets metamorphose into something quite different, and perhaps more benevolent in some ways, for instance? And are there not other examples? I'm not saying we should all walk with our arms reaching up in surrender to meet the Gruumsbaggians. I just want to point out that all of this concern may be unnecessary. What, may I ask, were they doing at the Mall of Freehold that was so dangerous to us? Nothing that we can identify."

Ghewen was very muscular and very tall. If he had stood next to a Gruumsbaggian, he would have come up nearly to its neck. When he toiled in the fields, he seemed to do the work of three men, and his eyes always seemed to sparkle with kindness and intelligence, even when he was lecturing the rest of the council. He was one of the two council members Jack liked best, along with Cynthia Browning, who was not only his great-aunt but also the oldest person on the council.

Ghewen always wore a neatly trimmed beard, and his complexion was the color of burnished walnut. This was because he had one black and one Oriental grandparent. There were no distinct races in Jamesburg anymore. In the early days there had been people of every race, but the Caucasians had been in the majority and had absorbed the others. The resulting melange was heavily Caucasian, but almost everyone was of mixed descent to some degree. Racism had become irrelevant.

Ghewen was probably one of the best-read people in Jamesburg. He seemed to know nearly as much about pre-Big Blue history as did Jack. Once, Jack had had a question which neither Harold nor Ferdinand could answer. He wanted to know why aircraft carriers were so important in World War II, and Ghewen, who knew a lot about military history, had been able to give him an answer. Ghewen's area of specialization was education. When he was not needed in the fields or repair shops, he taught the children of Jamesburg how to read and write and add.

He would soon teach the people of Jamesburg, young and old alike, something else—something other than the three R's. He would teach them that even such a kind, respected, gentle, learned man as himself could have a breaking point. The people of Jamesburg did not know he had one because nothing they had ever done had provoked him sufficiently.

***

On Gruums-Baag, the remaining human children were being told to prepare for their trip. All the teenagers had been cleared from the Gruumsbaggian home world, and now it was the

44

younger children's turn to pack their toothbrushes and clothes, their books and cassettes, their teddy bears and security blankets, all of which were copies of things the Gruumsbaggians had found on Earth. Under the guidance of their tall, yellow, blue-haired mentors, they dutifully cleared out the little cottages in which they had been raised and stowed their belongings on the space vessels that had been provided.

So appalled were the Gruumsbaggians at what they had inadvertently done to the human race that they had brought the collected human genetic material, what they were sure was the last best hope of the human race, not to one of the cold, forbidding, half-civilized outlying planets like Gornohath, or Tweeten, or Mokkrat, or Topea, or any of the other thousands of Gruumsbaggian colonies, but to Gruums-Baag itself. To the teeming heart, the pulsating soul, the intimate bosom of their galaxy-spanning empire. They had taken the remnants of humanity and kept them close, as if their proximity, like that of a teddy bear or a well-loved blanket, would nurture and comfort it. The Gruumsbaggians had scoured Earth for living humans, and, except for those in Jamesburg, had taken all they could find. The humans they had brought back to Gruums-Baag had been taken apart, cell by cell, and their genetic material had been manipulated and stretched and played with until, from thousands upon thousands of vats and bottles and artificial wombs, emerged legions of human infants.

The Gruumsbaggians had left the humans of Jamesburg alone as a kind of insurance. When they began taking humans back to Gruums-Baag, they wanted to be sure to leave a viable wild population of humans on Earth—just in case. So that even if things didn't work out with the genetic reconstitution and duplication procedures on Gruums-Baag, there would always be some humans left in the universe. The Gruumsbaggians knew that extinction was forever.

Of course, now that the genetic procedures had succeeded, it was no longer quite so important to the Gruumsbaggians that they leave the people of Jamesburg alone.

***

At Council Hall in Jamesburg, Councilor Barbara Noler rose to answer Councilor Ghewen. In attendance were Jack and Henry and Mayor Blanchard, and the twelve members of the council, which included both men and women from the ages of twenty-nine to seventy-six. The meeting had been called on a contingency basis, and the general public of Jamesburg had been excluded in an attempt to minimize panic. Jack knew all the councilors—it was impossible not to know, or at least recognize, everyone in Jamesburg. Everyone was dressed simply. Some wore homemade garments made from wool, while others wore clothes made of dacron, or nylon, or polyester. Whenever someone needed clothing, all they needed to do was visit the ruins of an old retail store, where there was plenty of clothing to be had for the taking. Synthetic fabrics lasted a long time.

Barbara Noler was a plain-looking woman who had been on the council for five of the previous seven years. "I don't think Desmond knows what he's talking about," she said. "Perhaps he's forgotten what happened a hundred years ago. You can stay here and wait for their polite treatment, but I'm all for going. If you want to wait to turn blue and die, fine, but I'll be in Kansas, or some equally distant place, thousands of miles from the closest Gruumsbaggian. Right now, mark my words," she said, "those Gruumsbaggians at the Mall of Freehold are doubtless preparing some horrible torture for all of us. I'm sure it will be even worse for those dolts who expect leniency from them."

Barbara Noler had never been quite happy. Despite all of the social pressure to mate and to have children, she had refused to marry. Actually, it had not been very hard for her to avoid marriage, since the handful of men the council had selected as eligible to marry her considered her shrill and sullen and insistent and wanted little to do with her. For in Jamesburg she didn't quite fit in. It was not that she was evil or bad. She was just different. Perhaps a small, isolated town like Jamesburg was not for her. Perhaps she would have been happier in a larger world, where she could have lost herself in anonymity. But there are some people who are unhappy no matter what their situation, and perhaps she was one of them. There have always been people like that.

Regardless of her true nature, Barbara Noler, like the rest of them, was trapped by the reality the past had shaped for them. And regardless of her rhetoric, there was nowhere else she could go, nowhere but the howling wilderness. So she stayed in Jamesburg, and stayed on the council, a harsh, aloof, and dissident voice. In some circumstances such a voice could be helpful with constructive criticism. But under the wrong circumstances, the personality behind such a voice could make things unnecessarily complicated for everyone else.

***

Russel Like

A few miles away, in the Mall of Freehold, which in its heyday had simply been called the 'Freehold Mall' by those fortunate enough to shop and work in its mighty corridors, four hundred Gruumsbaggians were busy putting the finishing touches in place. The holes in the roof had been patched; the wild animals and birds had all been expelled; and the floor and walls had been virtually rebuilt. The merchandise, which had been carefully manufactured on Gruums-Baag according to the most reliable blueprints Gruumsbaggian researchers could find, had been arranged on shelves in all the stores. And Gruumsbaggians were being trained as clerks. They would have to do, until there were enough humans to go around. Through the mall wafted the aromas of pizza, and cinnamon buns, and flavored popcorn, and french fries cooked in peanut oil, and whole hogs roasting over open fires, and stir-fried twigs.

And in the very center of the mall, where three of its great corridors came together, the Gruumsbaggians had constructed a huge pen. In the pen was a live hippopotamus, which munched on the leaves and grasses provided for it and occassionally wallowed contentedly in a mud pool. The Gruumsbaggians knew that every mall had its hippopotamus. No mall could be without one. They had learned of this fact from a book discovered in several dilapidated libraries scattered around the continent. The relevant passage had clearly stated: "As everyone knows, malls are never complete without hippopotami."

The Gruumsbaggians had failed to realize that this sentence had been written in a spirit of parody. The author of the statement had actually meant it as a wry commentary in a description of a mall near his house which, in its attempt to lure customers, had filled its corridors with the unusual and the exotic. But the

After The Blue

Gruumsbaggians had absolutely no conception of satire or irony, those being purely human devices. The Gruumsbaggians were relocating half the hippos in Africa to reconstructed shopping malls.

***

Back at Council Hall in Jamesburg, Henry was speaking to the assembled councilors. He was slightly nervous, because he was the youngest member in attendance, but he felt his help was needed to set things straight. He'd seen what the Gruumsbaggians were doing, and he thought Barbara Noler was taking things a bit too far. "I don't think what they were doing was really that bad," he said, shrugging his shoulders. "They were just moving stuff around. None of it really looked dangerous."

Barbara Noler scowled at him. "Well, we'll see how right you are."

"Maybe the aliens are here to help us," suggested Stephanie Zorick. She was in her early thirties, and had a thin, boyish body, limp, scraggly blonde hair, and always wore a pair of thick eyeglasses over her dreamy green eyes. Her specialty was canning and food storage. "Maybe they really know what's best for us," she continued. "What if they were trying to help us the last time? Maybe they somehow did help us. You know, some people think we're better off now than we were before."

Stephanie Zorick read a lot of science fiction. She had read every pre-catastrophe science-fiction book in the Jamesburg library. Once, she had even convinced her husband to take a trip with her forty miles to the north, by foot, so they could scour the ruins for more science-fiction books. They found few books in readable condition, but the trip was a success as neither of them was eaten by wild dogs. She had once written a science-fiction story, which Jamesburg's printer had published in the monthly newsletter, about the return of the Gruumsbaggians and how they saved the human race from certain extinction.

"I really must say I don't think that's likely," said Cynthia Browning. "They may not be here to hurt us, dear, but I would be extremely surprised if they were here to help us. What do you think, Tom?" she said to Mayor Blanchard.

"Well, I...I must say I have to agree with you," the Mayor said.

Cynthia Browning was nearly eighty years old, a small, gray-haired, clear-eyed woman. She was almost universally respected in Jamesburg. This was attributed as much to her acknowledged determination, intelligence, and good humor as it was to her similarity to her great-grandmother, who was one of the legendary founders of post-catastrophe Jamesburg.

"Yes, I agree that's true," Councilor Ghewen said. "They probably aren't here to help us, and the possibility exists that they're here to do us some harm. So perhaps it would be appropriate to come to some decision on a course of action? For all we know, the Gruumsbaggian army could be on its way here, but I don't really expect that. Maybe the most sensible thing to do would be to expect, well, to expect the unexpected."

***

In his command center orbiting the Earth, Farnstarfl, the Gruumsbaggian On-Site Director of the Earth Project, continued reviewing the vast pile of books, microfilms and videotapes which his minions had gathered for him. Even though he had not yet learned everything there was to learn about humans and Earth, he had decided to begin the project immediately. Farnstarfl thought there was no reason why the changes which the Earth Project entailed could not be implemented gradually, as the need for them became apparent. It would be unreasonable to wait until everything was known about human history, since they were always learning new things. Farnstarfl was learning to appreciate how enormously complicated human society had been and hopefully would be again.

Sometimes Farnstarfl thought human society had been like an exquisitely designed flaxzen-mour. Flaxzen-mours were little devices which Gruumsbaggians wore on their wrists. They had several moving parts, and served many functions. The flaxzen-mour relayed an enormous amount of information to the Gruumsbaggians: when it was time to eat, where they were located at any given time, where the closest lavatory could be found, and much, much more. They were complicated, although of course not nearly as complicated as human society. Farnstarfl knew that through a chain of events, the actions of one human could affect wheat prices, which would lead to food shortages, which would lead to political destabilization, which might lead to the deployment of troops from one side of the planet to the other side of the planet. That was how complex human society had been. Like an intricate flaxzen-mour, human society had literally thousands of working parts, each with its own peculiar function—beautiful in its complexity. What a terrible tragedy that the Gruumsbaggians, completely by accident, had brought that society to ruin. Farnstarfl thought about how satisfying it had been to take apart and put

After The Blue

"Well," the aide said, "the humans there already have a few cars and a simple railroad. It seems plausible that they have retained a good portion of the old knowledge and natural ways."

Farnstarfl was ecstatic. "Good! Good! They might be easier than the others to train in the old ways. Very good! This should make our task much easier."

As successful as the captive human production program on Gruums-Baag had been, the supply of humans coming from Gruums-Baag was really pathetically small, when one considered what needed to be done, and how many humans there had been before. After all, when a flaxzen-mour design called for twelve glubbens, and only three glubbens were available, the resulting flaxzen-mour could hardly be expected to work properly. The several thousand humans in the settlement would not bring Earth's population up to its old levels overnight, but they would be very useful. It would be necessary to see, in that little settlement, how degraded their way of life was from the way it used to be, before the Gruumsbaggians' first fatal visit. It might require a lot of work.

Farnstarfl's happiness was dimmed for a moment by a sobering thought. Once, when as a Gruumlet he put a flaxzen-mour back together after dismantling it, the thing hadn't worked properly, and he had to refer to a working flaxzen-mour for clues as to how to do it properly. But here, for the Earth project, how would he know? Where was the working flaxzen-mour to which he could compare the finished job?

He would just have to make do. He shrugged both his upper and his lower arms, and then went back to reading one of the Earth books. It was a fascinating book, and it shed some light on the society of the humans as it had been. He was just at the part where the secret agent, in bed with the blonde with the cascading hair and the magnificent figure, had been surprised by the evil one-legged subversive with the eye patch and his gang of bloodthirsty mercenaries. Farnstarfl sighed contentedly. He was finding his job quite enjoyable.

***

At Council Hall, the debate about how to react to the return of the Gruumsbaggians to Earth continued. "You're all treating this like some kind of game," Barbara Noler said, pointing at Ghewen. "You! You sit there hypothesizing about them: 'they might be this and they might be that.' It makes me sick. You're not living in the real world! You're just pretending! That's ridiculous!"

"Please try to calm down, Barbara," cautioned Cynthia Browning. "We have to speculate at least a little bit. I don't know that there's much else we can do at this point."

Barbara ignored Cynthia and turned to face Stephanie. "And you, with your stupid story! Oh, sure, the Gruumsbaggians are all going to come down to lead us to the City of Gold, to the paradise on the hill. Well, it's not going to happen!"

"Cynthia's right, Barbara," said Mayor Blanchard, interrupting her tirade. "Please try to calm down. This is a tense time for all of us, you know." He wiped the sweat off of his pudgy forehead.

"And look, Barbara, I don't know that there's really much we can do about them anyway," said Ghewen. "There are just a few thousand of us. And look what they were able to do when humans numbered in the billions!"

After The Blue

Barbara regarded Ghewen with undisguised scorn. "All right. I just hope, when they begin torturing people, you're the first ones they pick. I bet they have hundreds of spaceships on the way here right now just full of things to kill humans with."

***

Not long after that, the first of hundreds upon hundreds of additional ships did, in fact, leave Gruums-Baag for Earth, so laden with cargo that if they had been ocean-going vessels they would have been riding low enough for water to slosh over the gunwales. Of course, the cargo was neither weapons of mass destruction, nor tools of mind control, nor instruments of torture, nor devices intended to induce insanity. The cargo was thousands of laughing, crying, playing, rowdy, human children, and they were being treated with the utmost kindness by their Gruumsbaggian caretakers. When they fell down and scraped their knees, their Gruumsbaggian supervisors cleaned them off and gave them band-aids. When they sniffled with colds their Gruumsbaggian supervisors gave them tissues. And when the children asked where they were going the Gruumsbaggians told them, with pride, that their destination was Earth.

Curiously, the Gruumsbaggians had been successful in raising humans to their mid-teen years without warping them too much. This was because they had not made, as of yet, any concerted effort to force these humans to live in any particular manner. They had just taught them facts, and made sure they had adequate food and decent shelter and clothing. The children's acculturation came as much from one another, and from old movies and TV shows, as from the Gruumsbaggians.

Russel Like

The first ship was followed by another, and another, and another, and for several hours, as they streamed out of the planet's biggest spaceport, the skies over Gruums-Baag glittered with chrome.

***

Finally, after several hours of anguished debate in the building on Railroad Avenue, the councilors decided to do what the leaders of any other sensible group of six thousand people armed only with a few rifles, some shotguns, and simple chemical explosives would do when forced to confront a technologically advanced, galaxy-spanning empire that had once decimated their people and was once again poised at their doorstep.

Nothing.

They would ignore the Gruumsbaggians in the hope that they might go away. The Council would keep the return of the Gruumsbaggians secret so that the rest of the citizens of Jamesburg would sleep soundly at night.

They were in for a big disappointment, of course.

***

Having finished the book about the secret agent—it had ended quite happily, with the forces of evil vanquished and the agent making love to yet another beautiful woman—Farnstarfl turned his attention to one of the many microfilms he had collected. He attempted to load the film into one of the machines the Gruumsbaggians had reconstructed, but first he tangled the film, turning it upside down and nearly ripping it in half. It was very frustrating.

Finally, he shoved it, slightly crumpled, into place. It was a microfilm of every issue of the 1995 *Smithsonian* magazine, published over one hundred years earlier, and, amazingly, the microfilm was still legible! The humans had been skilled. More the reason to help them recover their lost glory.

After idly skimming through the film to see what the articles were about, Farnstarfl settled on one article and began to read. It was about the California condor, and how the humans had driven the birds to the very brink of extinction. The humans had wanted to save the birds, so they raised as many as they could in captivity. They fed the captive baby birds with hand puppets that looked as much as possible like adult California condors, so the baby condors would learn to recognize their own species, would not get too accustomed to humans, and would learn to live just like their wild ancestors had. The condors weren't even supposed to know they were being raised by humans at all. They were supposed to think they were being raised by other condors.

Farnstarfl marveled at the story the article told, because it had such implications for his very own Earth Project, and maybe even for that little settlement near New York City. If that sort of thing could be attempted for one earth animal then why not for another? But then, this thing about the condors was only fiction, unlike that book about the secret agent. Or was it the other way around? Farnstarfl kept forgetting. He'd have to check. The Gruumsbaggian mind just didn't work that way.

There was no such thing as fiction among Gruumsbaggians.

Chapter 4

"Now that's two cokes, four burgers, three orders of fries, and a sundae?" Sheila repeated, readying her finger to strike the right keys on the cash register.

"Yes, yes, that's right," said the Gruumsbaggian, looking down on her from the other side of the counter. With his lower right hand he grasped the hand of a small human child, who was no more than seven years old.

"That'll be twelve dollars and thirty-seven cents," Sheila said. The Gruumsbaggian handed her a twenty-dollar bill and she counted back the change. At first, it was interesting to deal with money, which she had previously encountered only in her history classes on Gruums-Baag. But by now, after three days of almost nonstop business, it had become merely tedious.

After the Gruumsbaggian had taken his order and brought the child over to one of the tables, there was no one left in line. Sheila looked out at the restaurant floor, which was now packed with Gruumsbaggians. Accompanying each Gruumsbaggian was a human child, but sometimes two Gruumsbaggians accompanied only one human. She was staring blankly at the cash register when Fred approached her from behind.

Fred was in a jolly mood. "Business is very good, isn't it?" he said, slapping Sheila lightly on the back with his lower left hand. He had not even had to put up any advertisements to attract customers, since the central planners on Gruums-Baag were seeing to it that other Gruumsbaggians working on Earth knew of the McDonald's and what it was for. The planners had assured Fred that he need not worry about advertisements yet, which was a good thing, since the television stations were not operating yet, and no one would have seen billboards because the highways weren't being used yet either. His biggest problem was that he was understaffed, still only having one employee, although even this was not a crippling obstacle, as his four arms enabled him to cook very fast when he helped out in the kitchen. Still, he hoped headquarters would send him some more humans soon. That seemed to be a problem everywhere on Earth—too many Gruumsbaggians and not enough humans. But that was all right. Fred knew that would change in time. And he was grateful to have the work. He had been unemployed for quite some time before finding work with the Earth Project.

Gradually, the Gruumsbaggians and the little children finished their milk shakes and french fries and hamburgers, cleared the garbage off of their tables, and trickled out of the restaurant. After the last customers left and they closed the restaurant down, Sheila became so agitated she almost felt like bouncing off of the walls. She wanted company. As nice as Fred was, the company of a four-armed creature from outer space was just not enough to keep a seventeen-year old human content. The previous few days Sheila had just spent near the restaurant, relaxing and waiting for the time when the other humans, the ones closer to her own age, would arrive at the McDonald's. She did not know it would be a while, for there simply weren't that many of them, and the Gruumsbaggians were opening not only McDonald's but also Kentucky Fried Chickens and Burger Kings and Hardee's and other fast-food restaurants around the globe. Now her restlessness had reached a critical mass, and she could not tolerate the thought of sitting around and waiting for the McDonald's to open again the next day. "Fred," she said, "would it be all right if I went for a walk to see the area?"

He simultaneously scratched his big red nose with his upper right hand and scratched his back with his lower left hand in a typical Gruumsbaggian gesture of contemplation. "Well, I don't see why not," he finally said. "Just so long as you're back by opening tomorrow."

So she set off down the new highway that stretched past the McDonald's. She didn't know where she was going, but she didn't really care. She had a feeling that a little exploration of the area might help her to find the answers to some of the questions she had been grappling with. She knew she wasn't going to get any answers serving Big Macs and McNuggets to Gruumsbaggians and little children. Besides, the restaurant was getting really boring.

After a little while the pavement stopped and gave way to a tangle of grasses and shrubs. She walked along the edge of the vegetation until she discovered a narrow dirt path leading into the forest beyond the scrub. Then she got onto the path and followed it into the woods.

***

After The Blue

Jack had been taking a late-afternoon nap, after a morning spent working in the fields and an afternoon playing softball, when his father shook him awake. "Ferdinand is here to see you," his father said.

Jack rubbed the fog from his eyes and sat up. "Ferdinand? Why?" He wondered what the senior historian could want with him now. One reason he liked the idea of history as his specialty was that there were hardly ever any emergencies to take care of. That wasn't the way the medical specialists had it. They had to grow accustomed to being roused in the middle of the night, although they were allowed to do less physical labor in return. And then there were the security forces, who sometimes were asked to stay up all night, and the electronics repairmen, who were very often swamped with work. But for a historian to be needed on an emergency basis—that was unheard of.

He changed his clothes and went downstairs where his mother was serving Ferdinand a cup of sassafras tea. "Jack, Ferdinand has something very interesting to tell you."

"That's right, Jack," said Ferdinand. He was a stout man in late middle age who was just beginning to lose his straight, graying hair. "Something's happened which I thought would never happen again. It seems we're not the only people left on the planet. They've brought a wanderer in."

Jack was astonished. It had been twelve years! And the implications! Maybe Jamesburg was not humanity's last redoubt, after all. He was so surprised all he could manage in response, at first, was a simple "Wow."

"That's right, a wanderer," Ferdinand repeated. "Thought I'd seen the last one when old man Rafferty showed up twelve

61

years ago." He was always called 'old man' Rafferty because he had been close to eighty years old when he blundered into Jamesburg. He had spent almost his entire life alone since his parents had known of no other humans but one another, and they had died when he was in his teens, leaving him all by himself. Miraculously, he had managed to survive in the wilderness, by himself, for decades. Perhaps less miraculously, he had not encountered a single other human being in a lifetime spent wandering from his birthplace in New Mexico to Jamesburg in New Jersey. He had been so ecstatic, so full of joy, at finding a whole community of human beings, and he hadn't spoken to anyone besides himself for so long, that he was virtually inarticulate at first when the people of Jamesburg brought him in. When he finally spoke, it had been to say, "I've been looking for you all my life." He had died two weeks later. He was something of a legend in Jamesburg.

"So, a wanderer. Does that mean we have to do something?" Jack asked. He tried to remember if the full historians had taught him anything about what to do when wanderers showed up.

"Yes, Jack, we do," Ferdinand said. "I know we haven't taught you yet, but frankly, we were going to teach you this procedure last because we thought it so unlikely another wanderer would ever turn up. In fact, I want you to do it. The way things are going, the next wanderer may not appear until after Harold and I are gone and you're senior historian." He finished his tea and said, "Thank you, Roberta. Well, Jack, let's get moving, shall we?"

When Jack was introduced to Sheila—for she, of course, was the wanderer—he was instantly moved at the sight of her. Perhaps smitten would have been a better word, although he didn't know it. She was a stranger, and he had seen only one stranger before in his life. While he didn't know, on a personal basis, every one of Jamesburg's six thousand inhabitants, he at least recognized them all. The earlier stranger had been old man Rafferty, but Jack had been a young boy at the time. Sheila was the first stranger he'd seen as an adult, and he didn't realize at first that he found her long brown hair, pretty face, and slender figure attractive. Initially he thought she was so striking because she was a stranger and therefore exotic.

Ferdinand told him how she had been discovered by a few young boys playing near the woods, and they had brought her to Railroad Avenue. Then they fetched their mother, who knew what to do. She took Sheila in, and knowing the protocol for dealing with wanderers, in turn fetched Ferdinand. In the meantime she seated Sheila in her kitchen and offered her a cup of sassafras tea.

***

After being brought to the kitchen of the house in Jamesburg, Sheila had sat patiently drinking her tea and contemplating this latest turn of events. She had found a human city, true, but it didn't seem quite like what she would have expected from the lectures and films and so on to which she had been exposed on Gruums-Baag. She wondered at possible explanations. Maybe this wasn't Earth, after all. Or maybe the Gruumsbaggians were just plain wrong.

"Well, hello!" Ferdinand said heartily when he entered with Jack, extending his hand to her. She took it hesitatingly, uncertain of what to do, and then tentatively shook it.

"Ah, nice to meet you," she said. It wasn't only a new experience for Jack. Sheila had never encountered a human being more than a few years older than herself. There had been a considerable human population on Gruums-Baag, but most of them were children. Sheila had, herself, been one of the oldest humans on the planet.

"So! You're the first wanderer we've had visit us in quite a while," Ferdinand said, smiling. "We're very glad to see you."

"Wanderer?" Sheila said. She knew the meaning of the word, but hardly felt her afternoon hike from McDonald's over the few miles to Jamesburg qualified her as one.

"Oh yes," Ferdinand said, chuckling. "It's the word we use for anyone who hasn't grown up here in Jamesburg."

"But what about the other cities, like New York, or Washington, or London, or Tokyo, or any of those places? You call the people who grew up there wanderers?"

"Yes, we do. After all, as far as we know there are more people here than there are just about anywhere else. We know for a fact that there aren't any in New York."

Sheila was growing more and more confused. In the geography class she had on Gruums-Baag, she had learned about the biggest cities on Earth. New York had millions of people, she had been taught. She thought back to her history classes on Gruums-Baag, but could not remember any 'Jamesburg' being mentioned in any of them. Finally she decided to throw caution to the wind, deciding that she would look stupid no matter what, and asked, "Please, can you tell me, is this Earth?"

Jack and Ferdinand regarded one another with expressions of mild astonishment, confusion, and bewilderment. "Well, yes, this is Earth," Ferdinand said, his earlier heartiness now replaced by a careful, overly cordial tone. "What made you think that it was not? And, if I might ask, could you tell me where you're from?"

After The Blue

Sheila had no way of knowing the truth would be regarded with any sort of suspicion or disbelief. "I'm from Gruums-Baag," she said.

It was at this point that Ferdinand excused himself and Jack and led Jack into another room. "Look, Jack," Ferdinand said when they were safely out of earshot of Sheila, "if those Gruumsbaggians hadn't been seen the other day, doing whatever they were doing, I'd say she was crazy as a loon. But now, who knows? I think we should just treat her as a normal wanderer and ignore where she came from. She may be insane. She may not. You caught that question about what planet this is, so who knows? Maybe she is from Gruums-Baag. Maybe she's even a Gruumsbaggian in disguise. So what can we do? If they want to kill us they'll have no problem. We'll just have to treat her like a regular wanderer."

"Um, right. And we have procedures, a probationary period to make sure she's not insane or anything, anyway, don't we?"

"Of course. You remember the stories about Jamesburg's founding right after the Blue. From Rosenthal's memoirs? Of course you do. We've gone over them enough."

Suddenly Jack felt that he wanted to be alone with Sheila. He wanted to make Jamesburg his to show to her. He realized that as much as he liked and respected Ferdinand, he neither wanted nor needed his assistance in this particular endeavor. "Well," he said tentatively, "then I think I can handle this alone. In fact, if it's okay with you—would you mind if I did everything myself?"

Ferdinand took off his glasses and rubbed his cheeks with his hands. "I don't know, Jack," he said. "You've never handled a wanderer before. Not that you've had the opportunity, of course."

"But don't you think she might be less intimidated by just one person? And didn't you say by the next time one shows up, I'll probably have to handle them myself anyway? Come on. I know what to do."

"Well, all right. But be cautious," Ferdinand said. He clapped Jack on the back. "Good luck. I'll speak to you later." Then he went out.

Jack did not want to believe Sheila was a Gruumsbaggian in disguise. He now began to realize he was filled with not only desire for her, but also an urge to protect and make her feel secure in Jamesburg. And he desperately wanted to believe she was sane. So he decided to take her at face value. He went back to the kitchen where she was sipping at the last of her tea and introduced himself. "I'm Jack, the apprentice historian, and it's my job to show you around, show you how we do things around here," he said.

"That's your job?" she asked.

"Yeah. I'm supposed to convince you to stay and live with us in Jamesburg. That's what we're supposed to do for all the wanderers." He did not think it was necessary to mention the period of screening she would have to be subjected to, even though the people of Jamesburg had excellent reasons for insisting on such a probationary period.

"Why do you need to convince me to stay?"

"Because we need more people. There aren't very many of us, and we need more genetic diversity. We're getting too inbred."

"Oh." Sheila was not terribly familiar with genetics. Most of the things she had been taught by her Gruumsbaggian teachers on Gruums-Baag emphasized things like Earth geography, history, and culture. She had never learned very much science.

"Anyway," Jack said, "would you like to start the tour?"

After The Blue

First, as Ferdinand had instructed him, he showed her around the town. He showed her Railroad Avenue, at the center of town, with the train tracks separating the two gravel roads. He showed her all of the buildings lining either side of Railroad Avenue, most of which were over two hundred years old, having been built around the end of the nineteenth century. He showed her Lake Manalapan at the northern end of Railroad Avenue, and he showed her all of the Victorian houses lining the tree-shaded streets jutting off of Railroad Avenue. He explained to her how they got some of their food from farming, but that plenty of it came from hunting and fishing: from the forest came deer and rabbits and wild turkeys; and from the lake and ocean came bass and crabs and shrimp and mussels and clams and perch and flounder. He showed her the train tracks which were maintained in two directions from Jamesburg, towards the open ocean and also towards Raritan Bay. Train lines had been maintained in these directions not only because the people of Jamesburg enjoyed their seafood, but also because they sometimes allowed themselves the luxury of a day's relaxation on the beach in the shadow of dilapidated hulks of rotting timbers and regenerating shoreline forests. He explained how the people of Jamesburg maintained a fairly large network of gravel roads. He showed her the central generator where logs were burned and turned into electricity which was carried into all of the houses through a grid, and he explained how most of the houses also had fireplaces so they could burn wood to heat themselves. He told her that they still had some functioning VCRs and computers, but their supply of videotapes was limited, although they did have a complete selection of *Star Trek* tapes. And while they had some working televisions, they were not terribly useful without VCRs because the only programs broadcast were on a cable channel which was produced entirely in Jamesburg and was usually sort of boring. He told her it was getting harder and harder to find working electronic equipment in the ruins of the old stores. They were having to go further and further away, and when the existing equipment broke beyond repair, it was feared that would be the last of the equipment for Jamesburg. But still, they did have some electronic equipment, and they believed this set them apart from every other human who might still be on the planet. He pointed out a few of the automobiles which had been salvaged and adapted to run on fuels derived from corn, and he stayed with her near the tracks for which Railroad Avenue was named while one of the trains chugged into town from the ocean, brimming over with the day's catch of crabs and mussels and flounder. He even showed her some of the farms and some of the buildings used for manufacturing and repairs on the outskirts of town, although he did not take her all the way to the auto maintenance facility in the Mall of Brunswick.

"So you see," he told her after they had finished the tour and were sitting on a bench overlooking Lake Manalapan and Railroad Avenue, "almost everyone has to do some of the physical work, like farming and logging and repair work, but if you have one of the more demanding specialties, then you aren't required to do as much. And almost everyone has a specialty. We try to make sure that at least three people have each particular specialty at any given time. When one of the specialists dies, the remaining ones have to teach a young person their specialty. That's how we've managed to preserve some of the knowledge and skills from before the Big Blue."

"The what?"

"Uh, well, you know, the catastrophe."

"What catastrophe?"

"You really don't know?"

"No, I don't. And I don't understand something else, either. You tell me this is Earth, and the Gruumsbaggians tell me this is Earth..."

"You...you've spoken to Gruumsbaggians!" Jack exclaimed.

"Well, so what's wrong with that?"

"After what they did, that you'd even go near them..." Jack exclaimed. He remembered she had said she was from Gruums-Baag. He wondered if she could possibly have been telling the truth.

"After what they did!" Sheila said. "They've never done anything to me. They've always been very nice." Then her expression turned uncertain. "But they must have lied about Earth. There seem to be hardly any people here at all. And you say they did something. What was it?"

"You were really brought up on Gruums-Baag?" Jack asked cautiously.

"Yes. And so were a whole lot of other people. But they always told us Earth was a place with millions and millions of humans, and no Gruumsbaggians. I've seen more Gruumsbaggians here than humans. I'm not sure what to believe anymore."

"So they never told you about the catastrophe?"

"There it is again. That word. What catastrophe? What do you mean?"

Jack realized he would have to begin with the basics. "It's

true, there used to be a lot of humans here. But the Gruumsbaggians came and wiped most of them out."

Now it was Sheila's turn to be shocked. "What happened?" she asked.

"There was an epidemic," Jack said. "They landed here, telling us they were just here on a peaceful visit, and they only stayed a few days. A few weeks later it was all over. There was hardly anyone left. The disease obviously came from them."

"Tell me," Sheila said, looking imploringly into Jack's eyes. "Tell me what happened. Tell me everything."

Jack found her gaze irresistible. And besides, it was his job, as historian, to know what had happened. He had read, and practically memorized, the written accounts left by Rosenthal before his death fifty years earlier. "I can tell you, if you have some time," he said.

"Please," Sheila said. "I want to hear it all. The Gruumsbaggians haven't been telling me everything. I'm so confused."

"Well, most of it comes from memoirs left by one of Jamesburg's founders," Jack began, looking out over Railroad Avenue, and he could feel himself being transported back into a past that was simultaneously remote and familiar. "A man named Rosenthal. He was about twenty-eight or twenty-nine at the time, and he'd been working in a computer distribution business with a few of his friends, not far from here, when it happened..."

Chapter 5

Rosenthal awakened the morning after Karen died, mildly shocked to still be alive, but caring little, because it seemed now absolutely everyone he knew was dead. Everyone. His family, friends, neighbors, absolutely everyone. He could not even remember the last living person he had seen before Karen. It was too numbing to grieve for any single person. All he felt was an immense emptiness. There seemed to be no reason to go on living. So he just lay in bed, numb and listless.

It had been a mere two and a half weeks, seventeen days, since the Gruumsbaggian visit to Earth. Their arrival had been final, irrevocable proof that humans were not alone in the universe, and had led to much fanfare among the public, and soul searching among theologians and scientists. It had also prompted spasms of millennial and apocalyptic fervor around the globe. A self-immolating human pyramid in Mexico City. The ritual slaughter of ten thousand yaks in Tibet. And so on. The Gruumsbaggians stayed just three days, and world leaders and others they chose to see found themselves traipsing to northern Manitoba, where the

Russel Like

Gruumsbaggians had landed and from which they showed an unwillingness to move. They just wanted to introduce themselves, they said, to get a glimpse of Earth culture, and then they would be off. But they would return someday. Moving around would be too risky, they said, with the ship they had. They might land on a populated area. What hypocrisy, Rosenthal thought bitterly, coming from the likes of them!

It had been two days after they took off that the first reports of the disease began to surface in the press. 'Mysterious Malady Strikes Entourages of World Leaders,' one headline had blared. When the Vice President of the United States, the Foreign Minister of Russia, the Prime Minister of Italy, and the King of Saudi Arabia all died within hours of one another, all of them separated by thousands of miles, it was apparent the disease could only be traced back to the visit with the Gruumsbaggian envoys. By this time, though, medical research was out of the question. The disease, or more properly, fear of the disease, had spread throughout the population, and no sensible medical researcher was about to brave the crazed, looting mobs ransacking the stores and terrorizing the streets.

This chaos had not lasted long, however; the disease itself spread only slightly more slowly than the panic it engendered, and within a week most of the mobs perished along with their leaders. The disease was horrible, in a surreptitious sort of way. It didn't make you feel sick in the least. It crept up on you and made you very tired, and then you fell asleep. You never woke up, although your skin did turn a ghastly shade of blue afterwards, perhaps from some chemical buildup caused by the disease. The whole process usually took no more than an hour or two. It was apparently spread through the air, but no one was really sure.

After The Blue

Rosenthal was wondering how much longer it would be until it was his turn to die when he realized he was hungry. He had not eaten in a day and a half. He roused himself out of the bed and dazed, as if in a dream, made his way to his apartment's kitchen. He opened the refrigerator and was greeted by a stale, fetid smell. He quickly shut it. Of course, the electricity hadn't worked for three or four days. The refrigerator must be full of sour milk and rotting vegetables. The suddenness of the collapse was perhaps the most disconcerting aspect of the entire affair. During the last few days during which there had seemed to be other people alive—although they were dying in droves—radio and TV stations simply stopped broadcasting, one after another, until there were none left. The last newspaper he had read had been printed a week ago. It had been a copy of *The New York Times*, and it had a full-page headline that said 'Still No Cure In Sight for Extraterrestrial Disease; Panic Spreads in Cities Around the Globe; Toll Now Placed at Two and a Half Billion.' There was a subheading, too. It read 'Corpses Pose Enormous Disposal Problem. Mass Cremations Urged.'

Finally he found some crackers and canned fruit in the pantry which he ate with little relish. Then he crawled back into bed to await his death. Eating had been such a futile gesture. The human race was finished, and he would be the last to see it go. He would die with grief and solitude his only companions.

He continued this twilight existence for several days, during which he finished all of the nonperishable items in his apartment but failed to show any signs of illness. Gradually it dawned on him that through some quirk of fate, or the luck of the genetic draw, he might have some natural immunity to the disease. He concluded the Gruumsbaggians had done a pretty poor job of genetically engineering a disease to wipe out humanity when it left some people untouched. Or perhaps, he thought, the Gruumsbaggians didn't mind if a handful of humans were left, so long as their civilization was virtually destroyed.

Rather than restoring him to good cheer, the realization that he had an immunity plunged him into an even deeper depression. What did he have to live for now that he was all alone? He contemplated taking his own life through more conventional means than the contraction of an alien illness, but decided this would be a pointless and futile gesture. That sort of thing was just not in his nature. And maybe there would be someone else left alive, after all.

Hunger was what finally prompted him to leave his apartment. He emerged into a world strangely devoid of all human activity. No airplanes buzzing overhead, no faint roar of traffic on the highway, no lawnmowers rattling away. Just a world of chirping birds and clear blue skies and corpses. His apartment building was in the suburbs, and the corpses were ubiquitous, but it was still possible to walk around without stepping on them. The peacefulness of the scene was overlain with the stench of decay. The world had turned into a charnel house. It was eerie, even terrifying, to be the only one alive amid so much ruin. But he became resigned to the reality of his situation, and after a day or two the corpses no longer fazed him.

He got into his car. It started and he drove the three miles to the closest supermarket, passing one car wreck along the side of the road that hadn't been cleared. A blue corpse sat at the wheel. Upon entering the supermarket, which was easy because the doors were all smashed, he was greeted by the stench of a different kind of decay, the decay of fresh meat and produce, of frozen dinners and sour milk. But what was left of the canned goods, the pastas, the crackers, the candies, the cookies, the cereals, the rice, and the bottled juices were all fine, and he took out as much as he could, covering his nose when he passed one of the handful of rotting blue corpses, some of them still in neat red uniforms, scattered around the store. He loaded his car and drove back to his apartment.

For the next few days he spent his time exploring the region. He visited the building from which he and his friends and partners had run their business. It was eerily vacant, and he did not stay long. He drove the fifteen miles from his apartment in Plainsboro to Rutgers University, where he had attended college. He did not stay long there, either, as the city of New Brunswick was packed with corpses and reeked of decay. He found that to be true of the other cities he visited, like Elizabeth and Trenton, in the hope of finding someone still alive. He learned to avoid the cities, to stay to the country and suburban roads. The action of driving itself was very easy. His was the only moving car on the roads, and though there were car wrecks in places, he could almost always get around them. There was plenty of gas to be had, of course. Most of the filling stations still had some stocks, and of course there was never anyone to charge him for it. It was fairly simple to siphon gas out of the underground storage tanks, and when that was not convenient, he simply siphoned it out of other cars.

It was not long before he learned of a new hazard awaiting him. On a whim, he had been investigating the vicinity of a pond hidden in some woods in the forlorn hope that he might find someone still alive there. He left his car at the nearest road and as he was walking back to it along a gravel path, a German shepherd, the collar still around its neck, appeared perhaps twenty feet in front of him. It looked emaciated, as if it had not eaten in a long time. As it stood there, snarling, he felt a visceral fear that he had never felt before, something primal, the fear a wild animal has of predators. He scooped up a handful of gravel along with a few larger stones and hurled them at the dog. Some of them glanced off the dog's muzzle. The dog was easily cowed. It slunk off with a whimper, and he ran to his car quickly, before it had a chance to regain its confidence.

Then he went straight to a gun shop and took everything—shotguns, pistols, ammunition, knives—that he thought might be useful. After that he never went anywhere unarmed.

During these few weeks he continued to use his apartment as his home base. He could have lived in any house he chose, of course, as there would have been no one to stop him. But he felt uncomfortable with the thought of moving into the house of someone who had just died. And he had already equipped his apartment for survival without utilities. He had a kerosene camping stove, a supply of flashlights and batteries, and plenty of food. He had even rigged up an outhouse of sorts, and he was able to bathe in a nearby stream which he hoped was not terribly polluted. He had not figured out how to heat the apartment yet, but it was only May. He would not need heat for a while.

Finally, after more than three weeks of completely solitary existence, during which time he had begun to abandon all hope of anyone else having survived the epidemic, he discovered another living human being. He was in the supermarket, a ShopRite—not the one closest to his house, which he had already emptied of the items he found most desirable—when he heard the noise of falling cans from the next aisle. Leaving the shopping cart he was stacking with cartons of canned corn and carrots, he readied his shotgun and crept towards the aisle.

He peered around a pile of paper towels, ready to shoot whatever dog or other animal had invaded the supermarket, but he was not prepared for what he saw. A teenage girl, no more than fourteen, with shoulder-length blonde hair and a face smudged with dirt, was trying to open a can of cooked pears with a can opener. There were several cans scattered around her feet. Upon seeing him she dropped the can and screamed, and then burst into tears. "Ohmigod, ohmigod, ohmigod, don't shoot me!" she said. "Please, please, I didn't even know there was anyone else alive!" And she sobbed again.

Rosenthal lowered his gun and strode over to her. "I...I'm so sorry," he said. It was odd to speak to another human being after so many weeks. "I've just had problems with wild dogs. That's why I had my gun ready when I heard some noise over here. But boy, am I glad to see you! I thought I was the only one left also. I'm sorry if I scared you."

She stopped sobbing and looked straight at him. "My name's Cynthia," she said with a sniffle, and he could see a smile begin to form at the corners of her mouth. She extended her hand.

"David. David Rosenthal," he replied, shaking the outstretched hand. "I can't tell you how...happy I am to know that there are other people out here."

As they drove back to his apartment in his car, they told one another their stories. Cynthia's father had been a physics professor at the local state college, and her mother had been a lawyer. Cynthia herself had just turned thirteen. Both of her parents had perished during the first few days of the epidemic. Her two brothers, ages seventeen and eleven, had lasted a few days longer than most other people but eventually succumbed. School, of course, had been closed within days of the epidemic's start in a vain attempt to slow its spread. Like Rosenthal, Cynthia had waited for the disease to come for her during the several days after everyone else she knew had died, but had shown no signs of sickness. She had been walking from place to place looking for people and living off of Twinkies and canned fruits ever since leaving her home. She said she was from Montclair.

"Montclair!" Rosenthal exclaimed. "That must be fifty miles from here!" Then again, she had had several weeks to walk the distance. But the fact that she had traveled so far without seeing anyone was ominous. She had walked through what had been a densely populated area without encountering a single living soul. While the trip might be testimony to her hardiness, as had her surviving the epidemic, it did not bode well for the future. But perhaps the extinction of the human race was not, after all, imminent. He took his eyes off the wheel long enough to glance at her nubile young body. She was pretty and slim, with a figure that was already quite mature. Just glancing at her was sufficient to arouse him. He had not seen a living woman in nearly a month. But she barely had both feet out of the cradle, he reminded himself. If they found no one else, then he would try to restrain himself for at least a few years. But, assuming she was healthy, he knew one thing at least: the human race would survive another generation.

It was almost a foregone conclusion that they would stay together. It did not take either of them long to realize how valuable the companionship of the other was in buoying their own spirits.

After The Blue

They set themselves up in an empty suburban ranch house with a fireplace that they found in an isolated, wooded area of Princeton Township, far from the stench of rotting corpses. The house, too, was empty of corpses. Rosenthal was forced to discard his car, a compact that was really too small for two people and all their supplies anyway, when its transmission failed. Instead, he took the car of one his neighbors at the apartment building. It was a large, sturdy station wagon, and it carried plenty of groceries and emergency rations.

They established a daily routine of sorts. They left the blinds open and got up with the sun. After a little while spent taking care of the house—they would trim the grass, shrubs, and other vegetation, and dust inside—they would drive around the region for several hours, visiting supermarkets and convenience stores, gathering as much nonperishable food as they could. Rosenthal always drove, as Cynthia was not yet inclined to learn, even though Rosenthal offered to teach her. While looking for food they would do their best to look for other living people. They decided that if they had both survived, others must have too, or at least they forced themselves to believe this. Their search for other people was limited, though, by the necessity of avoiding heavily populated areas because of the stench of decay.

"I tried to go to New York City," Cynthia said, "but it smelled real bad. I figured there might be somebody still alive there. I found a map, and I think maybe I was near Jersey City, or something, but I'm not sure. I turned around when it just got too horrible smelling. That's when I headed towards where I met you."

After their return to the house towards nightfall, they would have some dinner, perhaps read for a while, or play one of the several board games they had collected, then go to sleep. The nights were pleasantly cool and they had not yet begun to think seriously about what they would do during the winter. Twice, feral dogs ventured near the house, and they encountered a few on the road. Rosenthal shot them all.

They continued on like this well into July, during which time they established a warm but essentially platonic relationship. They discussed the subject of sex at one point. Cynthia brought it up, frankly admitting that she was strongly attracted to him, but he said, over his own physical urges, that he felt it would be healthier for her if they waited a while, that perhaps they might still each find someone closer to their own age. Besides, he realized they had an almost familial relationship. She looked up to him and he would have felt miserable taking advantage of her innocence. He would have felt something like a pimp, or some sophisticated city conniver, manipulating a young runaway for short-term pleasure. For the time being, her companionship was enough. The fact that she had survived suggested others might have as well, and this thought gave him immeasurable renewed hope.

Finally, in late July, they did find some other people. They found them in a place they had driven through once previously, at night. One evening Rosenthal was poring over the maps he had taken from a local 7-11, trying to determine which places they had visited several times in their search for other survivors and which they had missed. He had maps of the entire state of New Jersey, most of eastern Pennsylvania, all of Delaware, and the nearby regions of New York State. They were avoiding Long Island because it required travel through New York City, although by this time the stench was beginning to dissipate in some areas, with animals feeding on the corpses and the advance of normal decomposition. Finally, Rosenthal drew up a search plan. "Cynthia," he said, "tomorrow we're going to these places: Colts Neck, Red Bank, Rumson, and Jamesburg." And it was in Jamesburg that they found the elderly Mrs. Browning and her ten grandchildren, all still as full of vigor and life as anyone on the planet had ever been.

***

"Oh!" Sheila said excitedly as Jack paused for a breath. "So you're all descended from the twelve of them, from Rosenthal and Cynthia and the ten grandchildren!"

"No, no," Jack said. "My god, if it were that way, then we'd be even more inbred than we already are. They'd never let you marry anyone! No, there's more to it than that. Although you're half-right. One of Mrs. Browning's granddaughters was one of my great-grandmothers. And so was Cynthia."

"I want to hear the rest of it," Sheila said. She thought it was fascinating, being taught real human history by a human being. "Tell me more." She was so fascinated that she did not even bother to wonder why the Gruumsbaggians had never told her any of this.

Jack, however, was not listening. He was staring down Railroad Avenue in open-mouthed astonishment, for strolling down Railroad Avenue was a Gruumsbaggian. The alien was dressed, incredibly, in a blue human business suit which accommodated all four of his arms, a bright yellow tie, and a black top hat which completely hid his spiky blue hair. Jack knew of suits, but he very rarely saw anyone wearing one. Accompanying the Gruumsbaggian were several small, unfamiliar boys, all dressed in blue uniforms adorned with medals. Jack did not realize it, but they were wearing Cub Scout uniforms, or at least what the Gruumsbaggians thought that cub scout uniforms might have looked like. The Gruumsbaggian seemed to be directing the boys from house to house where they knocked on the doors, pulling little red wagons piled high with something almost, but not quite, transparent. The Gruumsbaggian seemed to scamper out of sight whenever a door was opened in response to the boys' knocks.

"Come on," Jack said, grasping Sheila's hand. "We really need to see what's going on. I'll tell you more about Jamesburg later."

Chapter 6

Jack virtually sprinted towards the Gruumsbaggian, dragging Sheila along with him. "It's just a Gruumsbaggian, Jack," Sheila protested. "It's really nothing to be worried about. They're not as bad as you think. They've never hurt any of us."

Jack stopped and looked at her curiously. "It really doesn't bother you, does it? Were you telling the truth before, about being born on Gruums-Baag?"

"Yes, I was. And they brought me to Earth, too, if this is really Earth. But I don't think they caused the disease on purpose. Maybe it was an accident."

"I don't really know anymore," Jack admitted. "Let's find out what's going on here." They had slowed down to a trot and were now almost at the Gruumsbaggian, who seemed not to be paying them any attention at all. Jack was uncertain how to proceed. From earliest childhood he had been taught that Gruumsbaggians were the incarnation of evil, and now this attractive girl said they had been kind to her. So he stopped to assess the situation.

Russel Like

One of the small boys, who was about nine or ten years old and was the second stranger Jack had seen that day, walked up to the porch of one of the houses on Railroad Avenue. The little red wagon he pulled behind him was packed with small plastic bags filled with water and tied shut at the top. In each bag swam a small goldfish. Upon reaching the door, he hesitated and looked at the Gruumsbaggian.

"Go on, Bobby, go on," said the Gruumsbaggian gently, bending over almost in half to bring his face closer to the child's. "We really need to raise this money for our troop. You've knocked on five or six doors already. This shouldn't be too hard." Jack noticed that the Gruumsbaggian, again, appeared to be careful to stay out of the sight of the door.

"Okay," said the little boy, although he was still visibly nervous. He rapped at the door two or three times, and after several seconds Mrs. Ernestine answered the door. This did not surprise Jack, as it was, after all, the Ernestines' house.

"Yes?" she said, apparently trying to remember just whose little boy this was, since he could not possibly look familiar to her.

"Um, hello, my name is Bobby, and I'm selling goldfish for the cub scouts?" he said in a high-pitched, querulous voice. "Anyway, would you like to buy some goldfish? They only cost two dollars each. We need the money so we can go to the convention in....oh, I forget..."

"Topeka," yelled the Gruumsbaggian from around the corner. Mrs. Ernestine looked confused, but just nodded her head. It was not only the apparently disembodied voice of the Gruumsbaggian that confused her. It was, among other things, the mention of money. Money was not used in Jamesburg. It allowed

84

too many opportunities for cheating and manipulation and theft and for people to do nothing at all. The people of Jamesburg could not afford that if they were to survive at some level of civilization. If you did not do your fair share of work in Jamesburg as long as you were able, you were exiled, and you did not eat.

"Yeah, in Topeka," said Bobby. "So will you please buy some goldfish?" He pointed at the fish in the bags on the wagon.

Mrs. Ernestine seemed to soften. "Look, Bobby, I'm afraid I don't understand exactly what you mean. Maybe you should find a different game to play?" Then she saw Jack. "Oh, hi, Jack! Do you know who his parents are?"

Jack looked at Sheila and then back at Mrs. Ernestine. "Sorry, I don't."

"Well, maybe you can help him find them?" she said, and shut the door.

Meanwhile Bobby had walked back to the Gruumsbaggian. "No one wants to buy anything," he complained. "They don't even understand me."

"That's all right," said the Gruumsbaggian. "Now just go to the next house and see if anyone there wants to buy some goldfish."

"Okay," Bobby said dejectedly, and, with his head down, began dragging his wagon to the next house.

"Do you understand what exactly is going on here?" Jack asked Sheila.

"Well, no, not really," she said. "Why don't you ask the Gruumsbaggian? They're not really that bad. Maybe they did some horrible things a long time ago, but they've never done anything bad to me or anyone I know."

"Well...okay. I guess if they're going to kill me, it'll happen no matter what I do. I won't be able to stop it." He strode over to the Gruumsbaggian. "Excuse me," he said, "but can I ask you what exactly it is that you're doing here? Don't you think you've caused the human race enough trouble?"

"Well, what we're doing here is, my cub scout troop, the kids, they all want to go to the annual convention in Topeka. But we don't have enough money from dues, so we have to raise money by selling fish from door to door. It's done all the time. You must have seen it before?"

It was almost as hard for Jack to believe he had gotten this sort of response as it was for him to accept having a conversation with a living, breathing, walking, talking Gruumsbaggian. "No. What I mean is, what are you, you Gruumsbaggians, doing here on Earth? I know you're not the only one. I saw a lot of others at the Mall of Freehold. So what are you going to do to us? Why are you here on Earth?"

"Gruumsbaggian? What a strange word! And, here on 'Earth?' I'm afraid I don't quite understand," said the Gruumsbaggian, as if Jack were speaking a foreign language.

Of course the Gruumsbaggian knew exactly what Jack was talking about, but he had his orders, which came down all the way from Farnstarfl. The orders clearly said that the Gruumsbaggians were supposed to be as inconspicuous as possible when among the humans, especially the humans of Jamesburg. They were supposed to play their roles to the hilt, even if it meant denying their Gruumsbaggianity. In this way the people of Jamesburg might come to accept them as...almost human. Like condor puppets. Thus the Gruumsbaggian had donned the suit, tie, and top hat, but unfortunately even these could not disguise the fact he had four arms, banana-yellow skin, blue hair, an oblong red nose, and was seven and a half feet tall. Even Gruumsbaggian technology had its limits.

"I just don't understand what you mean," continued the Gruumsbaggian, shaking his head. "My scouts have to keep trying to sell our fish. I think it would be really good for my boys to go to the convention. So if you'd please excuse me..." He walked away, followed by a small flock of boys in blue uniforms, fish-filled red wagons in tow.

Jack looked at Sheila in confusion. "Do you have any idea at all what's going on?" he said.

"Honestly, I don't think I've ever understood the Gruumsbaggians. They're very strange. But they're usually very nice. You should give them a chance. Anyway, I should be heading back towards work. I've really enjoyed the story, and I want to hear the rest soon."

"Work?"

"Yeah. At McDonald's? Fred will be waiting for me. He's a Gruumsbaggian too, and he's so sweet."

Jack's head was spinning. "You work for a Gruumsbaggian? You really do?"

***

On the way back, Sheila wondered if it were really necessary for her to go back to the McDonald's. The people in Jamesburg seemed nice enough, and they said they needed more people. Sheila wondered what it would be like to live in a place with just human beings. The thought was actually a little scary. But then she remembered Jack's story. Was it possible that the Gruumsbaggians had actually done that? It sounded awful. Everything was so confusing all of a sudden. That was really why she had decided to go back. It was just all too overwhelming. She needed to absorb it in a familiar place, and the McDonald's was the most familiar place available. Fred, however, would have some explaining to do.

***

The Gruumsbaggian cub scout master and his charges failed to sell a single goldfish in Jamesburg. This, of course, was not surprising, since no one in Jamesburg had any money. They did succeed, however, in confusing a number of people, including Mrs. Ernestine, and in panicking the few people who actually saw the Gruumsbaggian. No one but Jack had approached the Gruumsbaggian directly, as everyone else had been too frightened, but Jack had the coaxing of a pretty girl he wanted to impress and who did not seem the least bit afraid.

And at least some positive results had come out of the expedition, from the Gruumsbaggian point of view. The little boys were learning what it was like to be cub scouts, and the humans of Jamesburg were learning to accept cub scouts, just like they had in the past. It was all part of Farnstarfl's plan, that they should not go too fast but should begin to reacquaint the people of Jamesburg with their former way of life one step at a time, gradually, as if they were just learning to walk.

***

After The Blue

The visit of the Gruumsbaggian to Jamesburg transformed what had been the knowledge of just the council, the historians, and a few others—that the Gruumsbaggians had returned to Earth—into a subject of general knowledge. The feeling engendered among the people of Jamesburg was not so much one of panic as one of resignation, because if the Gruumsbaggians had wiped out nearly the entire human race once before, when humans numbered in the billions and ruled the planet, there was no way the people of Jamesburg could hope to resist them now. At least they were secure in the knowledge they were all immune to the Gruumsbaggian disease that had previously wiped out most of the human race.

Perhaps it would have given the people of Jamesburg some comfort if they could have known what had really happened when the Gruumsbaggian scout ship visited Earth a century earlier. It had been a deep-space scouting vessel which discovered Earth and landed there. Its crew did not know of any protocol for establishing contact with an alien race, because that had never happened to any Gruumsbaggian before. The Gruumsbaggians had in fact begun to suspect they were all alone in the galaxy. If the crew had included one of the Gruumsbaggian race's truly brilliant intellects some sort of precautionary measures might have been taken. But upon discovering Earth and its civilization, the crew were excited, ebullient, like little children on Christmas morning, and they tumbled out of their ship as soon as they landed on Earth without so much as a shower or a washing of the hands. It could have happened just as easily that humans carried a microbe which was fatal to Gruumsbaggians, of course; but that had not been the way things had worked out. And after the scouts returned to Gruums-Baag, and the consequences of their rash visit had become apparent, they were severely punished. They had been sentenced to fifty years' imprisonment in the derelict salt mines of the planet Ickor, where they had their right lower and left upper arms bound semi-permanently behind their backs. This was a great handicap for Gruumsbaggians, who have a hard time coordinating diagonally opposed arms. There they had been forced to repair broken flaxzen-mours six days a week.

***

A few days later, when he had some free time in the afternoon, Jack turned the television in his parents' house on, in part to try to forget about Sheila, whose place of residence he had not managed to find out, so befuddled had he been by the events surrounding her departure, and in part because he was curious to see what was on.

Ever since the visit of the cub scouts and their Gruumsbaggian leader the people of Jamesburg had begun to notice some additions to their television reception. Previously they had not gotten any channels on their hundred-year old TVs except for the locally produced Jamesburg cable channel. While every house had a TV, these were hooked up to hundred-year old VCRs and usually used for viewing old videocassettes. Now channels were broadcast around the dial.

There was one rather disturbing problem.

All of the TV shows featured Gruumsbaggians.

Jack flipped the channel until he came across an opening title which read 'At the Movies.' Cheery music played, and two

Gruumsbaggians, dressed in suits, came and sat down in what Jack recognized as an old-style movie theater auditorium.

"Hi, I'm Gene, and this is Roger, and we're here to discuss the latest movies," one of the Gruumsbaggians said.

"Good evening," Roger said. "This week's first movie is called 'The Affair of Gregory and Jean.' First, let's show you a clip."

The television screen zoomed into the movie theater screen on the television program, and Jack watched two humans, a young man and a young woman, apparently in a pre-Big Blue scene, talking to each other and going into a restaurant in a big city in the rain. "So what does your father do, Jean?" the young man asked as they were seated by the maitre'd.

"Oh, he's in banking," the young woman responded. "But he's almost ready to retire. He and my mother want to travel before they're too old to enjoy it."

A waiter came over to the table and put down a basket of rolls. He asked the couple if they would like anything to drink, and then left them to their conversation. They chatted for a while longer, and then the waiter returned.

The scene dissolved and was replaced by the two Gruumsbaggians, Roger and Gene. "So what did you think, Gene?" asked Roger.

"Well, Roger, I'm not sure I liked the restaurant all that much. The rolls seemed hard and stale. They had to ask the waiter for ketchup three times before he brought it over. And the fish, when it finally came, looked pale and flavorless."

"Okay, Gene, that may be true. But you have to admit that the decor was superb. Here they are in a seafood restaurant, and

91

they have all sorts of appropriate fixtures. There was an anchor on the wall behind them, and, if you noticed, when they entered, there was a captain's wheel from an old sailing ship! I think director Arthur Kardon has really outdone himself in this one."

Gene shook his long yellow head. "No, Roger, you're just not getting it. The service was horrible! I couldn't recommend this movie to anyone." Gene turned to face the camera "So there you have it, folks. A thumbs up from Roger but a big thumbs down from me. So let's move on to our next film. Here's a clip."

Again the movie screen expanded to fill the television screen and footage of a young man began to play. He was walking on a beach and he wore only a bathing suit. He approached a voluptuous, raven-haired woman in a bikini and said, "Hey, babe, how's it going?"

"Well, okay," she said, and giggled.

"What do you say you and me...you know?" the young man said with a wink.

The woman's brow furrowed. "You and me...what? I don't understand."

The film halted and was replaced by the two Gruumsbaggians. "Well, what did you think, Gene?" Roger said.

"You know, Roger, I'm of two minds about this film," said Gene. "On the one hand the woman was visually stunning."

"Yes! Yes! My thought exactly! But I also felt she was, well, conceptually banal."

"Right! Well, there you have it. We both agreed on this one. This film was visually stunning yet conceptually banal. And now on to our next film, a zany romp through old East Berlin."

Something about the movie reviews seemed very wrong but Jack wasn't exactly sure what it was. He had not yet gotten heavily into popular culture in his historical studies. He would have to research it. He flipped the channel, past advertisements for beer, cigarettes, and plastic ducks with unusually long necks that dipped their beaks repeatedly in glasses of water, until he came across a program which featured a Gruumsbaggian wearing a suit, tie, and fedora sitting behind a desk of some sort. "And now for the news!" announced a voice from off of the screen. "With your news, heeeeeere's Johnny!"

"Thank you, Ed," said the Gruumsbaggian behind the desk, glancing to his left. Then he picked up a sheaf of papers with his lower arms and began to read from them, his upper arms folded across his chest and nearly covering his tie. "In our first story of the day, thirty-seven people in London, England, were surprised by terrorists and messed up very badly."

The picture of the newscaster faded and was replaced by several Gruumsbaggians dressed in knickers, bowler hats, and polo shirts. The city they were in was identified as London by a logo at the bottom of the screen. Suddenly, as if from nowhere, Gruumsbaggians dressed as clowns ran into the crowd, hurling lavish cream pies in the faces of the other Gruumsbaggians, who screamed and covered their eyes. Then disembodied laughter flooded out the other sounds. There were chuckles, and snickers, and great, breath-defying guffaws.

Jack, now fully alert, stared at the screen. From some of the old videotapes he had seen, he knew what laugh tracks were. They were the part of the television show that told you how you were supposed to feel at certain moments. He could understand why the clowns throwing pies were supposed to be funny, but he was having a hard time figuring out why the Gruumsbaggians had decided to put this on the news.

As the Gruumsbaggians in knickers slowly licked the pie residue off of their faces, the scene in London faded out as the newscaster reappeared. "In other news, ethnic violence continued today in many places throughout the world," said the newscaster, shaking his big banana-yellow head. The newscaster again faded out, to be replaced by a picture of a city someplace Jack could not identify, except that he could recognize it was tropical because of the palm trees lining the street. Banana-yellow Gruumsbaggians were running up and down the street, along with purple Gruumsbaggians—or at least Gruumsbaggians that looked purple to Jack. He wondered if they had been painted. Whenever a yellow one encountered a purple one, it would knock the purple one to the ground and begin pummeling it. Jack could not hear what any of the Gruumsbaggians were saying because almost as soon as the yellow and purple Gruumsbaggians appeared on the screen, disembodied sobs began to emanate from the television set. The sobs seemed to have the same rhythm to them as the laughs from a few minutes earlier, as if someone had deleted the laughs on a tape and used the sobs to fill in the resulting gaps.

He watched for a little while longer, just long enough to see Gruumsbaggians described as the Presidents of the United States, Russia, and Great Britain shaking hands after signing some sort of pact. Then followed a short clip in which a Gruumsbaggian walking along a beach tried to explain just why everyone needed to purchase a special set of steak knives with which to cut dog food.

After The Blue

Jack felt he should be frightened. After all, these were the same creatures responsible for wiping out most of the human race. But, as after seeing them at the Mall of Freehold and talking to Sheila, he felt more puzzled than frightened. He could not imagine why they would be doing the things they were doing if they really planned to kill them all. He turned the TV off, stood up, and stretched. Then he went outside and blinked his eyes to acclimate them to the sunlight before heading towards the lake where he knew Henry would be fishing.

Henry was just reeling in his third bass of the day when Jack arrived. He brushed his shaggy red hair out of his face and said, "Hey, Jack, do you want to see something strange? Look at these fish." He pointed at his bucket.

Jack peered into the bucket. All he could see was the silver flash of tails slipping through the water. "So?" he said.

Henry reached a gloved hand into the bucket and plucked one of the fish out. "Look at this. Isn't this strange?" He was pointing at the fish's side, where a pattern in the scales formed the words 'Drink Budweiser Beer.' Also formed by the scales, above the words, was a picture of a beer can.

"An advertisement!" Jack said.

"Is that what it is? The hunting party today also found something like this on the deer they brought in."

"What? What did they find?"

"It was part of the deer's fur. It was a message that said, 'Smoke Marlboros For Better Taste,' and it had a picture of some sort of rectangular box. Do you know what those were? I guess the Gruumsbaggians are doing this, huh?"

***

Farnstarfl had realized that human society had been shaped by a number of forces. Therefore, it was necessary to recreate those forces, such as, for example, advertising, and resource constraints, and different political interests, and...and there were so many! There were environmentalists, and political lobbyists, and demonstrators, and other special interest groups, all of whom had reasons of their own for being. It was incredibly complex, but it was so much fun. And they were making progress in some areas, at least. They had begun to reintroduce advertising to Jamesburg, and Farnstarfl and his underlings were making plans to implement other aspects of the Earth Project.

Farnstarfl was dreaming of the moment, perhaps in a not-so-distant future, when Earth might be restored almost completely to its former glory, and Farnstarfl would order the final change which would make that restoration complete, when he was interrupted by an aide who rushed into his office and said, "Most high, we have a communication that you might find to be of interest."

"Yes? What is it?"

"The humans at the little settlement of 'Jamesburg' have historians. They must have much knowledge of the way things were before."

"Historians! Excellent! Excellent! More than we could have hoped for! We must speak to them as soon as possible. How did you find out?"

"Through one of the children living there. This child encountered one of our cub scouts and realized the child was a stranger. He said he had to get the *historians* to speak to the cub

96

scout. Apparently it is their procedure to introduce strange human beings to the historians. Our cub scout pack master overheard the whole thing. He thinks he may know who the historians are. He believes one of the Jamesburg children involved saw the two of them walking and pointed to them."

***

When Jack was told that Harold and Ferdinand, the two full historians, had been kidnapped by the Gruumsbaggians, he became quite nervous. He did not know whether to expect to be kidnapped next, or whether he should expect anything at all, so he was very careful whenever there were Gruumsbaggians in the street—which seemed to be happening more and more—to stay inside. No one knew what to make of the kidnappings. This was the first act of direct harm any of the Gruumsbaggians had made towards any of the people of Jamesburg, and it was very confusing. If they were going to kill the humans, then why would they do it piecemeal, one or two at a time? Some got the feeling, as a result, that the Gruumsbaggians were not out to kill them all; but others concluded that the Gruumsbaggians might be planning something even worse.

Besides being upset and worried about Harold and Ferdinand—he had, after all, worked with them quite closely— Jack wondered what the Gruumsbaggians might have in store for him. Was it something about historians? Did the Gruumsbaggians want to kill them all? Jack wondered if the Gruumsbaggians wanted to expunge any memory the humans had of the catastrophe, and perhaps thought the best way to do it would be by removing all of the historians.

97

Once, when he was in the house by himself, he heard a knock at the door. Forgetting for a moment that he was supposed to be afraid for his life, he answered it.

A Gruumsbaggian, dressed in a black suit and top hat, and carrying a briefcase, was standing outside.

Jack's heart began to pound uncontrollably. This was it, then. They were going to take him. His brief life seemed to flash before his eyes.

"Would you like to buy a yacht?" the Gruumsbaggian said.

"Would I what?"

"I said, would you like to buy a yacht? I'm a door-to-door yacht salesman. Surely you've seen door-to-door salesmen before?"

Jack felt a wave of relief sweep over him. Maybe the Gruumsbaggians did not even know he was the apprentice historian. But what had this one said? A yacht? Jack strained to remember if he knew what that was.

"They're very cheap," said the Gruumsbaggian. "Only fifty thousand dollars. You could sail it on the lake over here. It's a limited time offer, so you better hurry."

"Um, I don't think I'm interested," Jack said.

"Are you sure? I could come in and show you some pictures. I have them here in my briefcase. I think you might change your mind! You might be making a big mistake!"

"No, no thank you," Jack said, closing the door over the Gruumsbaggian's protest of 'Come on. I'm having a very bad day.' He closed the door too quickly to see the Gruumsbaggian referring to his script to see if he had, in fact, said the right things in his role as a door-to-door yacht salesman.

***

After The Blue

Up in his orbiting command center, Farnstarfl was very pleased. More ships carrying human children were arriving from Gruums-Baag, and the Jamesburg operations were going smoothly. The humans there were gradually getting accustomed to the way things used to be. Soon it would be time to proceed to the more essential aspects of pre-epidemic life. Door-to-door salesmen and television programs were all well and good, of course, and they were parts of pre-epidemic life that needed to be reconstituted, but there were so many more aspects! It was time to move on. The interrogation of the historians, who had been captured and brought to a regional control center in New York City, was providing much insight into the ways of the humans of Jamesburg.

Farnstarfl had plowed further through his pile of books, videotapes and microfilms. By a happy coincidence he had come upon both the book and movie versions of 'The Invisible Man' almost simultaneously. At first he had been quite concerned, because he had not been aware humans could make themselves invisible, and he wondered if there were more humans on Earth than the Gruumsbaggians actually saw. Then he ordered the captive historians to be questioned about this, and their assertions that this was definitely a work of fiction made everything much clearer. Then he marveled at the imagination of the human who had concocted it. Since fiction was alien to Gruumsbaggians, no Gruumsbaggian had ever made up any sort of story at all. But now Farnstarfl was intrigued. If humans could make up stories, then why couldn't he, a reasonably intelligent Gruumsbaggian, do the same? So he set himself a challenge: he would create a sequel to the *Invisible Man*, and the sequel could be shown to the humans on Earth. Sequels had apparently been a big part of pre-epidemic culture.

He had even picked out a theme and a title for the first sequel. He would call it *'The Inaudible Man.'* It would be about a man who could not be heard, and who, like the invisible man, tried to use his special ability to take over the world. Even thinking of the idea made Farnstarfl feel very pleased with himself.

After the 'Inaudible Man,' who knew? He wondered if there might be a story behind 'The Unsmellable Man.'

***

The next day Jack was summoned to an emergency council meeting. Harold had turned up and was briefing the council, and Jack's attendance was desired. When Jack arrived at Council Hall, Mayor Blanchard said, "Harold, here, has been telling us what it is he thinks the Gruumsbaggians are doing."

Harold looked slightly disheveled but not too bad for one who had been a captive of creatures as horrible as the Gruumsbaggians. He told Jack how the Gruumsbaggians had taken Ferdinand and himself to a building in New York City, where they had been asked an endless series of questions about Jamesburg's history. Apart from the questioning, though, they had been treated decently. They had been given adequate food and water, and they had even been provided with beds and with time to sleep on them. Finally, after several days, the Gruumsbaggians said they were done with them and released them near Jamesburg. Ferdinand, who was a good deal older than Harold, had not come to the meeting because he was tired after his captivity, despite the relatively lenient treatment they had received, and needed to rest.

"So what is it the Gruumsbaggians are trying to do?" Jack asked when Harold had finished.

"Well," said Harold, "I'm not certain, but I think they might be trying their best to recreate the society that was in place when they came and ruined everything."

"But why?"

"You see, I gather that it was an accident."

"An accident! That was some accident!"

"Yes. They didn't realize they might carry a disease to which so few humans would be immune. And they seem anxious to recreate what they destroyed. Why, I'm not really sure."

"But how are they going to know how things were? We're not even sure of everything."

"I gather that's one reason they took Ferdinand and me. They grilled us for hours and hours, often about things we just couldn't answer. They seem to be relying primarily on old books, videotapes, microfilms, things like that."

"That's why we needed to call you here. We need to discuss responses to this, and they may have to be history-based," said Mayor Blanchard. "At least it's a relief to know they're not here to slaughter us. All right, then. Does anyone have any ideas? I, for one, don't necessarily want to live *exactly* like they used to. Not that the Gruumsbaggians are accurate in what they're doing. I assume you've all heard about the advertisements on the fish. Anyway, I just don't think the old ways would suit us exactly, any-more."

There were murmurs of agreement from the assembled councilors. "You say they're going to be using books to figure out how to recreate what we once were like?" Ghewen asked Harold.

"Yes, that's right."

"Well, then I think the answer is clear. We write books and put them on microfilm. The printers can do that, so the Gruumsbaggians take these as authentic and act accordingly. We might have some wonderful opportunities here!" said Ghewen.

"I agree, Desmond," said Cynthia. "That's a marvelous idea."

"Oh, yes," Barbara said. "A huge empire that spans the galaxy, and we're going to fool them with a couple of books. Who do you think you're kidding, Desmond? It's just not going to work."

"I'm not so sure about that. If we don't try, how will we know? There are apparently a lot of Gruumsbaggians around here willing to put a lot of energy into this endeavor. If we can channel that into a direction that's beneficial to us, why shouldn't..." He stopped in mid-sentence and turned his gaze towards the door, which had begun to shudder. Everyone else followed his gaze.

With a loud crack the door popped off of its hinges and three Gruumsbaggians, leaning down to avoid hitting their heads on the doorframe, burst into the room. They headed straight for Harold. One of them grasped him with all four arms, and, as effortlessly as if he were lifting a doll, carried Harold out of the room. Beyond the doorway, Jack could see another Gruumsbaggian carrying Ferdinand, who seemed to be struggling futilely to escape the alien's hold. "Farnstarfl wants to see them," one of the other Gruumsbaggians said to the council, almost apologetically. Then they were gone.

The meeting broke up soon afterwards, without any real policy decisions having been made. Jack had reached some conclusions of his own, however. He was wondering if it was too late to choose another, perhaps less dangerous, specialty.

After The Blue

Farnstarfl had been rather aggravated when he learned that the Jamesburg historians had been released. Then his aides reminded him that he himself had given the go-ahead for them to be freed, and he sullenly countermanded the order. "Bring them up here this time! They are too valuable to let go!" He was secretly hoping they would help him with his screenplay for 'The Inaudible Man,' with which he was having more difficulty than he expected. He had been unable to figure out exactly how the ability to not be heard would help a human take over the world. So far he had only been able to figure out how it would be a hindrance. For example, how would a human order his meals at McDonald's if he couldn't use his voice to communicate? He couldn't point at the menu, because it was sort of far away, and the cashier might think he had picked the wrong item. Farnstarfl was begining to realize this 'storytelling' business was quite complicated.

But his movie was just one aspect of the Earth Project. There was another reason he wanted the historians at his side: the project was about to enter a new, more critical, and more detailed phase.

***

The next morning Jamesburg awoke to a drastically altered landscape. All of the forests had been chopped down for miles around. Only isolated trees were left standing every few hundred feet. A sign had been affixed to each of the remaining trees: 'Do not cut. By order of the Governor.' Huge billboards had been erected on much of the deforested land. Most of them featured pictures of

Gruumsbaggians holding cigarettes, or beer, or standing next to artificial plastic ducks with long necks which were dunking their beaks in glasses of water. The billboards had captions which urged readers to buy the products shown.

There were other changes, too. Next to the lake a huge, olive-green box had been deposited. It was the size of a house, and pipes jutted out from it here and there. It was apparently a machine of some sort, because it puffed and wheezed and gargled incessantly. From one of the pipes at the top emanated a dark, acrid smoke which, rather than rising, crept along the ground and collected in clumps all around town. From a pipe at the other end, a black, oily, viscous fluid spilled into the lake. Next to the machine was a big sign. It read: 'No fishing or swimming. Water severely polluted.' Other signs reading 'No hunting within thirty miles' had been placed all over town. 'Regulations enforced by the Governor.'

By mid-afternoon some of the smoke clumps began to rise, and by late in the day they nearly blotted out the sun. The clumps that rose were replaced by new smoke from the machine. Two Gruumsbaggians marched through town putting up more signs. The signs read 'Do not exercise. Air pollution alert.'

And there was one other thing. Nearly all the farmland, which had been plowed and carefully readied for the spring's planting, and, in some cases, was already green with tender shoots, had been paved—not with the gravel the people of Jamesburg used to pave their roads, but with seamless, unbroken asphalt.

When the council staged yet another emergency meeting, the mood was the grimmest it had been yet. The unpleasant black

smoke fouling their air and their lungs was the least of their problems. The councilors wondered, now that there were no trees,
, what would they would use for fuel. They wondered, with pavement instead of farmland, and a Gruumsbaggian prohibition on
hunting and fishing, what they would eat. They wondered how
they would survive.

They needn't have worried.

The Gruumsbaggians were going to give them jobs.

Chapter 7

Later that morning, when the people of Jamesburg were still grappling with the question of how to survive without fuel or food, Sheila came back into town. She had failed to get any satisfactory answers from Fred about the current state of affairs. She had in fact concluded that Fred did not know much except how to operate deep fryers, prepare milk shakes, and place orders for cartons filled with little packages of ketchup, so she had decided to return to Jamesburg. She hoped to hear more from Jack about the town's founding, and she was wondering whether she should go back to McDonald's at all.

On her way she wondered why the trees she passed before had now been replaced by stumps. She wondered if that was the way trees were; one day they were towering columns of brown and green, and within a few days they transformed themselves into squat cylindrical mounds. It was not so easy to explain away the smoke. As she approached Jamesburg, it grew harder and harder to breathe. At one point a deer, with the words 'Smoke Camels for

After The Blue

Better Taste' spelled out in its fur, bounded in front of her, but she was too busy coughing to pay it much attention.

Finally she got to Jamesburg. The dark gray smoke that hung over the town like a dirty blanket rendered it barely recognizable, but once she saw Railroad Avenue she knew she was in the right place. She asked the first person she saw if they could help her find Jack.

"You came back!" Jack said when they met. "So how is your Gruumsbaggian?"

"Oh, well, he...he's not very helpful. He doesn't know very much. I really want to hear the rest of your story. That's why I came back. But why...why is there all this black stuff here? This...this smoke?"

Jack pointed to the machine near the lake. "That thing," he said. "Courtesy of the Gruumsbaggians. And did you see what they did to all the trees? And the farmland? You still don't think they're so wonderful now, do you?"

"I...I don't know what to think anymore. I just want to know what happened. Please, can you finish the story now?"

He found her just as alluring as he had at their first meeting, and he would have done anything to please her. He had plenty of time, because he was scheduled to work in the fields that morning, and the Gruumsbaggians had made that impossible. "I'd be happy to," he said. They sat down on a bench on Railroad Avenue, on the other end of town from the lake and the smoke machine, and Jack, after reviewing Rosenthal's memoirs in his mind for a few moments, began to speak.

***

107

Russel Like

The morning after Rosenthal had identified several towns on his map as places they had not yet thoroughly searched for signs of human life, he and Cynthia drove to Jamesburg. Rosenthal had heard of Jamesburg while attending Rutgers, since it was not really that far away, but he had never visited the place. Cynthia, being much younger and coming from much further away, not surprisingly knew nothing about it at all.

"This is an odd-looking place," Rosenthal said, as they drove down East Railroad Avenue. "They have two streets called 'Railroad Avenue' and train tracks between them? I guess the name makes sense then."

The town was not one of New Jersey's suburbs. It had a real downtown lined with bakeries and hardware stores and groceries and luncheonettes, and the side streets were filled with tasteful, elegant Victorian houses. But it was evident that the town's heyday had passed. Several of the most attractive houses had been turned into funeral parlors, real estate agencies, and insurance offices. Jamesburg at first struck Rosenthal as the sort of declining Main Street town that could be found anywhere in the United States. Still, the town was more appealing than many they had seen. There was little evidence of the riots they had found in other areas. Very few windows were smashed, and the ubiquitous corpses were strangely absent.

It was Cynthia who spotted the people first. Normally, while Rosenthal concentrated on driving, she scanned the landscape for even the remotest indications that a living person might be nearby. "David!" she said excitedly. "Stop! I think I saw a little boy!"

"Where? Where?"

"Back there!" She pointed. "On the right! In the backyard in between those two houses. A little kid. Maybe five or six years old. And, I'm not sure, but I think there maybe was another one with him."

Rosenthal stopped abruptly and turned the car around. Driving, at least, was one activity that had grown more pleasant since the epidemic. He had not had to obey a traffic law for a long time. He had been able to speed, make illegal U-turns, pay no heed to 'yield' signs, and, in the spirit of an extreme libertarian's fondest dreams, completely ignore traffic lights, which no longer worked anyway. "Let me know when to stop. Where did you see them? Here?"

"Yes! Right here! Stop now!" she said breathlessly, barely able to contain her excitement.

Rosenthal stopped the car in the middle of the street and they both got out. "This way," Cynthia said. She led him across the railroad tracks that separated the two parallel downtown streets. Then they went down the narrow grassy strip between two of the old Victorian houses. As they got closer to the backyard, Rosenthal could hear the unmistakable sounds of little children at play. "I'm a little teapot/short and stout," they heard a whiny nasal voice shout, then dissolve into giggles.

"Tag! You're it!" another high-pitched voice yelled. Rosenthal and Cynthia looked at one another with expressions of mingled incredulity and hope.

As soon as they emerged into the backyard the children froze. There were three of them: two boys, one of whom looked about five or six, while the other appeared slightly younger, and an even younger girl, with short red hair in pigtails. She was wearing overalls. For a moment only the gentle clanging of distant wind chimes broke the silence.

"Hello! Hello!" a voice came to them from the other side of the yard. Rosenthal turned and saw a thin, elderly woman rise up out of a lawn chair and begin walking slowly towards them. Her wispy hair was completely white, but her eyes seemed to sparkle with intelligence and humor. She was dressed plainly, in blue slacks and a white blouse, and she wore a pair of wire-rim spectacles. "You two are the first people I've seen, other than my grandchildren, in months—ever since those Gruumsbaggians and their disease. I can't tell you how pleased I am to see you." She approached them and extended her hand. "My name is Rita Browning."

***

"So you and your grandchildren survived?" Rosenthal asked, after they had gone inside one of the Victorian houses, where Mrs. Browning insisted on serving them tea heated with a kerosene stove, along with some cookies salvaged from a local convenience store. The three little children were playing with some wooden blocks in the next room.

"I don't know you at all," Mrs. Browning said, "but I suppose I really have no choice but to trust you. After all, we really have no one else, do we? It's not like it was before, when you could afford to be suspicious of strangers." She spoke in soft, measured tones, and listening to her Rosenthal felt immediately that he was in the presence of a person of considerable wisdom and determination. "Yes. All of my grandchildren survived, thank God," she said,

110

in response to his question. She sighed, and her face assumed a more melancholy expression. "But their parents, my daughter and son and their spouses, weren't so fortunate. I have wondered about that, so I have read everything I could find about genetics. It doesn't appear surprising that resistance to a disease should skip generations like that. After all, it happens with hair color. Please excuse me for being pedantic. I taught general science in the junior high school here for thirty-five years, so I already have some familiarity with biology. Anyway, this is something to which I have given quite a bit of thought."

"Where are your other grandchildren?" Cynthia asked. "And how old are they?"

"Oh, they're around." Mrs. Browning nodded toward the toddlers in the next room. "There are ten. These here are the youngest," she said. "The older ones are out looking for food and other useful things. They'll be back later. One of the older ones is a boy you might like to meet, I think. I'm sure he'd like to meet you." She smiled gently, and Cynthia blushed but returned the smile.

"I realized something a little while ago," Rosenthal said. "Everywhere we've gone, except where there weren't any people to begin with, of course, there have been corpses. But I haven't seen a single one, not even a skeleton, here in Jamesburg."

"Oh, yes," Mrs. Browning said. "When it became clear it would just be the eleven of us here, I had the kids, the older ones, do their best to collect all the bodies and burn them, or at least burn the ones they couldn't move. The smell would have been horrible! Not to mention the disease hazard and the scavenging animals they'd have brought. Oh, yes, very early on we burned them all.

111

Even the ones we knew personally. That was a little more difficult, but it had to be done. Carted them off in red wagons and the like to the edge of town and just burned them. I couldn't do it myself, I just don't have the strength, but the kids had plenty of energy for it. No, central Jamesburg is completely free of bodies. This may sound strange, but I still take pride in the way this town looks. I was born and raised here, so were my children and so, God willing, will be my grandchildren. I won't have it looking like a mausoleum if I can help it."

Rosenthal was impressed. He had not had a small army of teenagers at his disposal, but still, he had made no attempt to clear bodies away. He had simply avoided them. This was further evidence of this woman's steadfastness in adversity and plain good sense.

"Have you given any thought to the winter?" he asked. "We can't expect to have heating gas pumped into our houses anymore. I've considered going south, to Florida, maybe."

"Yes, I have thought of that as well. But you know what? I've lived here all of my life, all eighty-one years of it. And I know, at my age and in my condition, without my husband, I wouldn't survive for more than a few weeks away from Jamesburg. I draw a certain strength from the familiarity of my surroundings here. And the children, especially the younger ones, still need me. They'll be all right here. The winters aren't all that bad. This isn't North Dakota. And anyway, we can take as many coats and blankets as we need from the stores, and a lot of the houses around here have fireplaces. Who's to stop us from taking some firewood? Very soon there will be vast forests all around here, if what you say about how few people are left in the rest of the world is true. I'll tell you what," she said, leaning over her tea and grasping each of them on the wrist, "you're both welcome to come and live here. In fact I'd love it. I think it would do the children some good to have a community again. Not to mention what it might do for you two. And this place is clean, like we discussed, no corpses anywhere. And it's sort of cozy. You might grow to like it."

Rosenthal considered what she had said. A community. Of course. If he and Cynthia, and this woman and her grandchildren had all survived, there obviously had to be other survivors, somewhere, other humans who were resistant to the disease. They could begin to build, right here on either side of Railroad Avenue, a new beginning for themselves. It would be much better than just trying to eke out a meager and semi-solitary existence off of the wreckage of the old world. Out of the ruins of that world they would begin to forge something better, perhaps, something that took the best elements of that world and rejected the worst. Combined with what Mrs. Browning said, it all added up to a captivating vision. "You're right," he said. "We'll move in. We can build something up here. We'll find others and bring them here, too." He warmed to the vision as he spoke of it. "We should rescue whatever knowledge and information we can," he added. "We need to preserve as many books, microfilms, things like that as possible."

"What about people who know things?" Cynthia said. "Like doctors and scientists. Shouldn't we get them too?"

"Yes, yes!" Rosenthal said, growing more excited. "We need to find as many specialists as we can. Let's see. We should try to find a doctor, an auto mechanic, and someone who knows something about agriculture and, oh, we'll have to make a list."

Russel Like

Mrs. Browning touched him gently on the hand. "I just hope we can find some of these specialists in the first place, David, if there are really as few people left as you say," she said, "but I consider myself an optimist. So let's take the optimistic view. Assuming we can find any of these people at all, let's try to have some redundancy among our experts. It will give us something to shoot for. What if we find a doctor, but then something happens to him, for example? We should really try to find at least two, if we can."

"It'll be just like Noah's Ark!" Cynthia said. "We have to find two doctors, and two carpenters, and two of everything."

Rosenthal held his hand up. "Well, Rita's right. We have to assume that we'll be lucky if we find anyone at all," he said. But still, he was truly enthusiastic. Starting a business with his friends, he had felt a sense of purpose and usefulness, but that seemed almost meaningless when compared to the venture he was planning now. He would have the opportunity to build the foundations of a new society, free of the tyranny of the past, free of the fetters of slavish conventions, free of the petty hatreds and vendettas bequeathed by history. He would have a hand in selecting those aspects of the past which would be preserved and which were worth preserving. It gave him a giddy sense of power and contentment. It also gave him a nearly overwhelming sense of responsibility.

***

After Rosenthal and Cynthia had relocated to Jamesburg and brought all of their personal possessions and hoarded food there, the thirteen of them began to make preparations for their search for other people. Mrs. Browning supervised the younger children in the cleaning of the houses, the storage of all the food they had scavenged, and in other tasks suited to their small hands. None of Mrs. Browning's flock knew how to drive, and Mrs. Browning herself said she had not driven in about fifteen years, so Rosenthal taught the oldest of the grandchildren, a fifteen-year old boy named Ted, how to drive, which wasn't difficult since it was no longer necessary to obey traffic laws. Ted and Cynthia struck up a youthful romance, which in a sense gratified Rosenthal, but also in a way made him feel lonelier than ever, since he and Cynthia had forged a special bond during the period when they felt they might be the last two people left on Earth. He consoled himself with the hope that somewhere, out in what was left of America, he might find someone for himself, someone closer to his own age.

By the first week of August, they were ready to begin their search. It was a hot, humid day, and the clothes stuck to one's back. But the days were getting shorter, and Rosenthal had begun to worry about the winter. And there was something else to be concerned about. To date all of the canned and packaged food they had been eating was fine, but the previous day they had opened a can of asparagus only to find it rotten. They hoped this was an isolated incident, since they had not found any other rotten canned vegetables, but Rosenthal feared it was a harbinger of things to come. Therefore they would have to begin making preparations to grow their own food. That would be easier once they established a real community with enough people to ensure a division of labor and a sizeable workforce, and when they had found some people who knew something about farming or canning. That can of rotten asparagus probably lent their task more of a sense of urgency than any can of rotten vegetables had ever lent to any other enterprise in history.

Rosenthal and Ted set out in a minivan they had found, which seemed like the optimum vehicle for their trip. Before leaving, they bid a fond farewell to Cynthia, Mrs. Browning, and the other children, but not before making sure the older children knew how to use guns against any feral dogs. Then they got onto the New Jersey Turnpike and began driving north. The plan was to explore the northernmost areas first, perhaps as far as Toronto and Maine, before the weather really began to change.

Before they found any living humans, they encountered a problem with the roads. Occasionally there would be a car wreck, usually with a corpse in an advanced state of decay behind the wheel, but these were easy enough to drive around. And potholes seemed to have proliferated in the absence of maintenance, although Rosenthal wondered about this, since there had been no frost yet, and the roads had obviously had no traffic recently. But the biggest hazard by far were collapsed overpasses and bridges. Most of the overpasses they traveled beneath were still standing, but there was one on the northern edge of the New Jersey Turnpike that had collapsed and lay in a heap of rubble across the highway. They got around it easily enough on side roads, but to Rosenthal it was emblematic of the decay, of the wilderness that would inevitably close in around them, of the total collapse of civilization. It reinforced the resolve he had gotten from seeing the can of rotten asparagus, and it made him more determined than ever to salvage what he could and build something out of the wreckage while there was perhaps still time. He did not want to become like one of those people he had seen in end-of-the-world movies who

116

lived all alone in dismal caves with only twelve cats for company and grew shaggy and incoherent. He wanted to have a life; he wanted to have children; and he wanted them to have lives too.

It was not until they reached Providence, Rhode Island, that they encountered another living human being, a woman in her early sixties who had worked for many years as an accountant. They welcomed her, of course, and she was happy to have found other people, but Rosenthal was somewhat disappointed. While her knowledge might be useful, and the more people they had the better off they would be, she was certainly not a mate for him, and she could not have children. Next, they managed to locate three people who had previously banded together in the Berkshires—an artist, a professor, and a college student. In this manner, they found almost thirty people throughout New England. Rosenthal gave them maps they could use to get back to Jamesburg and they would either agree to meet back in New Jersey or decide to accompany Rosenthal and Ted. It was easy to convince people to come with them. People were hungry for the hope and companionship offered by the prospect of a community. They only encountered two people who unconditionally refused to come to Jamesburg, but they accepted instructions about how to find Jamesburg anyway. Gratifyingly, they did not encounter anyone whom Rosenthal would not have wanted in his community, which struck him as odd, because it seemed to him that the pre-epidemic world had been composed of both pleasant and unpleasant people. Perhaps it was that they were all united in grief and hatred of the Gruumsbaggians, or perhaps it was the effect of isolation on people.

Finally, just as the leaves were beginning to change color, Rosenthal and Ted led a caravan of nine vehicles back to

Chapter 8

"War?" Sheila said. "With who?" Then she coughed.

She had interrupted to ask this question because Jack himself was busy coughing. "I really can't talk much more right now," Jack said after he had managed to catch his breath. "It's this smoke." Sullenly, because he did not like disappointing her and because, like the rest of the people of Jamesburg, he was preoccupied by the question of how they were going to survive without fuel or food, he gazed at the machine next to the lake.

Suddenly he was filled with the urge to tell Sheila how he felt about her. He wanted to tell her he had fallen in love with her the moment he met her, that he wanted to spend the rest of his life with her, and that the thought of being permanently separated from her was horrifying and would make life unbearable. But he was not quite sure how to go about doing this. He had read about things like this in old books and had seen it in old movies, but to actually do it was another thing. All his life he had been prepared just to approach girls who had been told to expect his approach by the council and the geneticists. But Sheila—Sheila was different. She had been

119

raised by Gruumsbaggians. Who knew what they had taught her to expect? And he had a lingering worry about what the council would say. The thought of a liaison that wasn't sanctioned by the council went against everything he had been taught. Sheila would certainly be sufficiently unrelated to him to be marriageable, although there could be other concerns. But he wondered if any of it mattered anymore. Things were changing in Jamesburg, and when he looked at the machine next to the lake, he wondered if life would ever be the same. But still, the matter of his feelings for Sheila was too important to botch. He would have to wait.

That didn't mean they couldn't continue to spend some time together, though. Jack inhaled, then breathed out slowly. This gave him the strength to talk a little more. "Would...would you like to take a walk?" he asked. "I could show you some more of Jamesburg."

"I would like that," Sheila said. "I would like that a lot. I want to see more of Jamesburg. I'm thinking that maybe, well, maybe I won't go back to the McDonald's."

Jack stopped to look at her. "I really hope you decide to stay with us, Sheila. We really need you," he said.

She said nothing, but her gentle smile made Jack's heart sing.

They strolled onto one of the side streets. In places the swirling smoke was so thick the houses were virtually invisible from the sidewalk. They passed a few humans as well as a few Gruumsbaggians. One of the Gruumsbaggians was dressed in a dark blue outfit and a peaked blue cap. Around his waist was a belt with a holster which held a pistol. With one hand the Gruumsbaggian held a sort of club and in another he had a small box with an antenna that squawked with voices and static.

"I think he was supposed to be a policemen," Jack said after the Gruumsbaggian disappeared into the smog.

Soon they came to the edge of town, where there had been fields until the Gruumsbaggians paved them over. It was difficult to see very far, but as they drew closer, a cacophony of sounds became audible. There were hammering noises, and drilling noises, and the noise of voices shouting to one another. Through the patches of smoke flashes of movement, of bright yellow skin and chrome machinery, were visible.

After they had walked a few hundred feet onto the asphalt-covered fields Jack realized what was going on. The Gruumsbaggians were putting up buildings on the pavement. Then it became apparent that they had already erected a number of buildings there. The first one they came to was a squat rectangular structure with a big flashing sign on the front. The sign read: 'Vito's Italian Restaurant.' Attached to the window in front were two pieces of paper. 'Lunch Menu,' one said, and the other said 'Dinner Menu.'

"Italian Restaurant?" Sheila said. "What's that?"

"It was...they were...I mean, I guess it's a place where they serve Italian-style food,"Jack said. He began to read from the dinner menu. "Let's see. There's eggplant parmigiana, and veal scallopini, and...and fettuccine alfredo, and..."

A Gruumsbaggian emerged from the front door. He was wearing a white smock and a big white chef's hat. "Good day, sir and ma'am," he said. "Would you care to come in? We have a special today. Spaghetti and meatballs with garlic bread for two. Only nineteen-ninety five." When he spoke, he attempted an Italian accent, but he did a very bad job, and even if he had been

121

successful, neither Jack nor Sheila would have recognized it for what it was.

For a moment, when he realized the Gruumsbaggian was offering them food, Jack thought that perhaps the Gruumsbaggians had not been as malicious in what they had done as he previously thought. Then he heard the part about the price. "I'm sorry," he said. "We don't have any money."

"No money? Then I'm very sorry, we can't serve you. Perhaps you should get jobs, no?" He went back inside and slammed the door.

"Hey! I think I'm supposed to get paid at McDonald's some time," Sheila said. "I wonder when that will be?"

But before she could say any more they were engulfed by a cloud of smoke and both of them coughed uncontrollably for several minutes.

After the smoke cloud passed by, they continued their exploration. Near Vito's Italian Restaurant they discovered Zorba's Greek Restaurant, and Vladimir's Russian Restaurant, and Tevye's Delicatessen, and Fidel's Cuban Restaurant, and Adolph's German Restaurant. And then they came across Bambi's Deer Restaurant.

"That's odd," Jack said.

"What is?"

"Well, the other restaurants were all ethnic restaurants. But this?" He peered at the menu which, just as at Vito's, was taped to the window.

After The Blue

Bark		$ 2.75
Saplings:	Oak	$ 4.98
	Pitch Pine	$ 5.37
	Birch	$ 3.94
Grass (heaping plate—enough for two):		$12.98

He didn't read any further. He did not know whether to laugh or to cry. He realized, whether they liked it or not, they were going to live under the reign of the Gruumsbaggians, who apparently had very little understanding of the way the world had worked. He wondered what it would be like.

"Sheila," he said, "I'm beginning to get a very bad feeling about all of this." His feeling was not improved by the sight of Rocky's Squirrel Restaurant, which served thirty-seven varieties of acorn, or Bugs' Rabbit Restaurant, which served mostly lettuce, or Kermit's Frog Restaurant, which served flies and mealworms.

The Gruumsbaggians had put up other structures besides restaurants. There was one building which bore the title 'Gun Shop.' Jack and Sheila wandered inside, and the Gruumsbaggian proprietor did not bother them. The merchandise included a wide variety of guns, not all of which Jack was able to identify. If Jack had been knowledgeable about twentieth-century weaponry, he would have recognized something that looked much like a Kalashnikov rifle, and something that resembled an Uzi submachine gun, and something else that looked just like a Saturday-Night Special. There were other things Jack could not identify at all. These were hand grenades, and canisters of nerve gas, and bazookas. And taking up one corner of the store was a reasonable facsimile of an inter-continental ballistic missile. These Jack pretty much ignored, but when he went over to admire the guns, the Gruumsbaggian proprietor rushed over and began telling him about the prices. They did not stay long in this store, but wandered past other stores with names like 'Cooking Store,' and 'Bread Store,' and 'Yogurt Store,' and 'Video Store.'

They went briefly into a store called 'Electronics Store.' There Jack saw all sorts of things the people of Jamesburg had dreamed about finding for decades. He saw sparkling new computers, and photocopiers, and printers, and camcorders, and videocassette players. He guessed they were all in working condition. After all, the televisions in the store were all working, albeit with Gruumsbaggian programs, one of which seemed to be a talk show on which the guests were introduced as 'eight middle-aged accountants.' Jack realized one of their two greatest problems, the increasing difficulty of finding serviceable electronics, had been solved by the arrival of the Gruumsbaggians. They would have access to new and plentiful electronic equipment. Then he looked at Sheila and remembered that their other great problem, the problem of too few people and low genetic diversity, might be solved too.

But then he looked outside at the roiling clouds of black smoke drifting by, and the Gruumsbaggians milling about in blue uniforms, and the farmland covered with asphalt, and thought about the machine pouring a putrid black goo into the lake, and the forests replaced by billboards advertising beer and cigarettes, and he wondered at the price they would pay for the solutions to these problems. He recalled that the very spot on which he was standing had been a lush green field beneath a clear blue sky as recently as the day before. Now it was a dreary expanse of pavement and buildings and the cheery sunshine of a late April morning had been replaced by a horrific black miasma which all but blotted out the sun.

That afternoon Jack was summoned to attend the council meeting. After the last week, he was actually getting accustomed to attending council meetings, which he had only gone to once or twice before in his whole life, and then as an observer. They had told him, though, that with the other historians gone, he was needed, because the time had come for Jamesburg's passivity in the face of the Gruumsbaggian onslaught to end, and his knowledge would be crucial.

The first order of business at Council Hall on Railroad Avenue was a discussion of the most recent developments. Someone had managed to rig up some sort of air filter for the room, so they all inhaled deeply upon entering. After he gulped in his fill, Mayor Blanchard called the meeting to attention by banging his shoe on the desk. "This meeting of the council shall now come to order!" he shouted. "First, I would like you all to hear an account of what's happened since we last convened this morning to discuss the paving of our farmland and the fouling of our air. Martin, if you would?"

Councilor Martin Oversee, a short, trim middle-aged man, stood up and began to read from a notebook he held. He told how Harvey Farelo-Wong and his two sons had ignored the signs prohibiting hunting and gone out after deer that afternoon; how they had succeeded in bagging a deer and were hauling it back to Jamesburg when they were accosted by four Gruumsbaggians in

125

blue uniforms; how the Gruumsbaggians had burned the deer car-
cass and forced the three men to accompany them at gunpoint,
telling them all the while that they should have known hunting was
prohibited because there were signs up and how violations of the
law could not be tolerated; how the Gruumsbaggians brought the
three men to a building labeled 'police station' which had been
constructed on one of the cornfields; and how the three men had
emerged from the building half an hour later covered with tar and
feathers but otherwise unharmed. The three men were currently
resting at home, Oversee said, where they were being plucked.

Councilor Oversee also had another incident to report.
George Ernestine had been walking down Railroad Avenue on the
way from his house to the lake—he wanted to get a closer look at
the mammoth Gruumsbaggian machine there—when a Gruumsbaggian, dressed in a black shirt and pants and wearing a black
mask over his eyes, jumped out from a side street and threatened
him with a knife, demanding his credit cards. George Ernestine was
at a loss at first, not remembering what credit cards were, but then
he was saved, ironically, by the gang of four Gruumsbaggians in
blue uniforms. They had taken this Gruumsbaggian away. Several
hours later the Gruumsbaggian who had accosted George was spotted along Railroad Avenue, recognizable because he still had the
black mask over his eyes, but *he* was covered with tar and feathers.
George was a bit shaken, but otherwise unharmed.

"So there you have it," said Mayor Blanchard. "We have to
do something. We know approximately what it is that they're trying to do. We know they're not here to kill us. They seem to be here
because, for whatever reason, they feel it to be their responsibility
to make us live like our ancestors used to, or like they think our

126

ancestors used to. That's why they've kidnapped our historians. We have to make sure that they don't learn that Jack knows something about history, too, because otherwise they may try to get him, and we're going to need his knowledge more than ever. Maybe they actually regret what happened a century ago. That doesn't matter. They're not human, and they seem to have made some big mistakes about how it was that we used to live, before the catastrophe. For example, Jack, how long has it been since anyone was tarred and feathered?"

"I'm not sure, but I know they weren't doing it for at least a hundred years before the catastrophe."

"There you have it. And if that's not enough evidence for any of you, just go walk around those restaurants they've put up. I took a stroll over there before the meeting. I'm sure none of you has any desire to eat just like an octopus does.

"Unfortunately, for a time, at least, we will have no choice but to go along with them. We have enough food supplies to last a few weeks at best. Hunting and farming are obviously not viable short-term options. And they do seem to be supplying some food that will be edible."

"But they're charging money for the food!" One of the councilors protested. "How are we supposed to pay for it?"

"You haven't heard?" Said Cynthia, smiling wryly.

"Heard? Heard what?"

"Desmond, could you..." she said.

"Certainly. Here we go." He hoisted a pile of newspapers from the floor to the table and began passing them out. "You may not have all seen this. The Gruumsbaggians were leaving piles of these around town today."

Jack began reading the cover of his copy before he had even taken it from Ghewen's hand. It was titled 'The Jamesburg Employment Opportunity Press,' and it was subtitled 'Over Six Thousand Jobs Available. Earn Money Now!' Jack leafed through it. It was full of descriptions of jobs. There were descriptions of jobs for dogcatchers, and firemen, and consultants, and chefs, and attorneys, and physicians, and many other jobs. There were also, scattered among the job descriptions, a few articles. One of the articles was entitled "JFK: The Truth Is Finally Out About the Assassination." Another article was entitled "Elvis Spotted in Madrid; Some Suspicion That He May Have Been With Amelia Earhart." And on the back cover, there was a note. It said, 'Anyone wanting one of these jobs should report to the lake at 9 A.M. tomorrow.'

"So you want us to get jobs from the Gruumsbaggians?" asked Barbara, with considerable astonishment.

"I don't think we have much choice in the short term," said Mayor Blanchard. "Either we work for them, or we starve to death."

"Or we all get tarred and feathered," said Ghewen. He shuddered. "Pleasant punishment, isn't it? There's a lot I'd endure before I'd let them tar and feather me."

"So we're supposed to just work for Gruumsbaggians," said Martin. "I can imagine what that will be like."

Mayor Blanchard held up his hand and smiled. "Remember, I said we don't have much choice in the short term. That's why, without Harold and Ferdinand, we need Jack. There is a way to thwart them. I think we may even have mentioned it before. Desmond, would you care to explain? It was, after all, your idea originally."

128

"Certainly. We know the Gruumsbaggians are getting their idea of what life on Earth used to be like from old books and newspapers and the like. What we have to do is to convince them, perhaps through a book we write ourselves, to leave us alone."

Jack was intrigued. "How are we going to do that?" he asked.

"Ah, that's where we'll need your help," Ghewen said. "I know a lot about history. As you know, it's been a hobby of mine, but there's still a lot I don't know. I'll help you where I can and so will some of the other councilors. But what we have to do is make sure what we write coincides sufficiently with what the Gruumsbaggians have learned from their research."

Councilor Adriane Lowarnd chuckled. "Like how tarring and feathering is a common punishment?" she said.

"Oh, yes, I can see this is another wonderful idea," Barbara said, shaking her head slowly back and forth.

"Well, Barbara," said Ghewen, "I haven't heard any other ideas from you. If you're not interested in helping, then you don't have to. But I'm getting rather exasperated with your unceasing criticism of everything we try to do here on the council. At least please try to be cooperative. Or would you rather join the Gruumsbaggians out there?"

After the council meeting adjourned, Jack, Ghewen, and several other council members got together and began discussing the book they would write. They discussed what they would say about Jamesburg, and just what it was they wanted the Gruumsbaggians to think. While they did not establish any specific outline for their book, they did manage to agree on some general principles.

And they were certain of their goal: to get the Gruumsbaggians to leave them alone, to let the people of Jamesburg live their lives as they had always lived them. Finally, around four o'clock in the afternoon, they assigned to each person present some specific tasks to work on for the book and agreed to meet again whenever possible the next day.

***

Up in his orbiting command center, Farnstarfl had come across a fascinating document. It was called *"The New Statistical World Almanac Fact Book,"* and it provided much new information about the state of affairs on pre-epidemic Earth. The statistics seemed particularly useful, and he wished he had come across them earlier. There was one statistic that said two percent of the pre-epidemic population had been criminals. He did some quick calculations and discovered that meant there should be one hundred and twenty criminals in Jamesburg. But as far as he could tell, there were very few criminals in Jamesburg, unless you counted the three who had gone hunting deer. Then he reminded himself to put in an order to Central Planning on Gruums-Baag for more tar. Those two Jamesburg historians insisted that tarring and feathering was not a normal punishment, but Farnstarfl could tell that while they were useful at times, they did not know everything about life on pre-epidemic Earth, and sometimes he would just have to go with the information his researchers provided.

He looked back at the lists of statistics. Ten percent of the population were homosexual, divorce rates had been thirty-seven percent, forty-nine percent of the people disliked, mistrusted, or hated people different from themselves, and so on.

130

After The Blue

This information was crucial to the restoration of Jamesburg to something like a normal state. The reforming of Jamesburg was a challenge, while the construction of a proper society with the humans from Gruums-Baag would be much easier, he believed. The humans of Jamesburg seemed so set in their incorrect ways, but he and his Gruumsbaggians would be able to twist and bend them back into shape. He knew that someday the humans there would be grateful.

He summoned the two historians back into his chamber. It was really quite useful to have them around, even if they weren't always accurate. At his bidding, they were teaching him how to play a human game. Farnstarfl had learned that games had been an integral part of Earth culture, and concluded it would be invaluable to have humans teach him how to play one of them. They had actually begun the game several days earlier, but it had been taking a while, so they had put it aside. Now Farnstarfl wanted to finish it.

"So you still want to continue with this?" Harold asked when he and Ferdinand were ushered in. "You just landed on my Boardwalk with four hotels. You can't afford to pay for that." If Farnstarfl had had a better feel for human intonation, he would have realized that the two historians, who had previously been very diffident in his presence, were growing more and more flippant as they came to realize he did not intend to hurt them.

"You already took a ten thousand dollar loan from the bank," Ferdinand added. "You can't take anymore until you pay it back. Are you sure you don't want to do something else?"

"Yeah," Harold said. "Like take us back to Earth?"

Farnstarfl looked at the two humans and then back at the Monopoly board. He tried to remember the rules again, and decid-

131

ed that they were probably right. He had lost. But he wasn't ready to send them back yet. He still needed their help, and there was so much more to learn. From under his desk he pulled out a set of Parcheesi. "I need to learn this one," Farnstarfl said, and the two humans groaned.

***

It was later that day that Jack got the bad news about Ghewen. Not long after they had finished working on the book for the day, Ghewen was out walking among the new buildings and stores the Gruumsbaggians had constructed on the old farmland. He was walking near something called the 'Kwik Convenience Milk Mini 6-10 Mart' when he found himself surrounded by four Gruumsbaggians in blue uniforms. Such bands seemed to be pro- liferating all over Jamesburg. One of the four handed him a pistol and ordered him, at gunpoint, to go inside the store. Once inside, they required him, still at gunpoint, to hold the pistol up to the Gruumsbaggian proprietor of the store and demand all of the cash in the cash register. When the proprietor surrendered a huge wad of green bills to him, the four Gruumsbaggians told Ghewen he was a criminal and they would have to place him under arrest and subject him to punishment. The observer's account had become murkier at this point, but somehow either the Gruumsbaggians had allowed Ghewen to escape, or he had managed to escape on his own. Ghewen had last been seen running as fast as he could away from Jamesburg.

Jack became depressed upon hearing about Ghewen. He had been counting on Ghewen's help in the writing of the book to fool the Gruumsbaggians. Now he wondered if Ghewen would

132

even feel safe returning to Jamesburg. The whole affair sounded very strange, but then, so did everything else the Gruumsbaggians were doing. He was also depressed because, while he thought Sheila had remained in Jamesburg, he had not been able to find her since getting out of the meeting. He needed to speak to a friend, so he went looking for Henry. Henry was in a foul mood.

"Do you know what happened to me today? Do you?" he said when he saw Jack.

"How am I supposed to know, Henry?" Jack answered, mildly surprised his friend was so upset. "I've been busy all day. But I'd like to know. Is it the pavement? The pollution? That affects us all, remember."

"I was just walking down the street when one of those Gruumsbaggians comes up to me and tells me I better not have any-thing to do with any girls, because I'm going to have to be a homo-sexual. It's not as if I was in such good shape before, with the geneticists giving me a choice between Debra and Mary, but now! And you know what they're going to do to me if I don't listen to them? Do you?"

"I can imagine," Jack said, thinking how Henry would look covered with feathers. "But what can you do about it?"

Neither of them yet knew Henry would eventually be tarred and feathered by the Gruumsbaggians, but not because of anything he had to do with Debra, or Mary, or any other girl.

Henry's face clouded over. "I've been doing some think-ing about this," he said. "You've heard about Ghewen, right? How he left town? I think I'm going to go looking for him. He's strong and smart, and I think if anyone can beat these Gruumsbag-gians, it's him."

"I know what you mean. I was just working with him at the council, and, well..."

"Right. I'm going to join him. Jack, do you want to come with me? I've heard about all these plans to go work for the Gruumsbaggians. That doesn't sound too appealing to me. Think about it! You, and me, and Ghewen, and whoever else comes, fighting the Gruumsbaggians from the wilderness!"

Jack wondered if there were any wilderness left or if the Gruumsbaggians had cut it all down. Henry's vision was sort of tempting. Then he thought about the council's need for him, without the two historians, and now without Ghewen, who had a more compelling reason to run away than Jack. It really seemed like their best chance for thwarting the Gruumsbaggians lay in the writing of the book. "I'm sorry, Henry," he said. "I'd love to, but I've made a commitment to the council. I can understand if you do it. I hope it works out. Try to let me know how it's going, okay?" He clapped Henry on the back and said goodbye.

Then Jack went home, where he discovered that blue-uniformed Gruumsbaggians had been assigned to both his mother and his father. Each one's Gruumsbaggian would hover over them and follow them everywhere they went. He first saw this when his mother greeted him at the front door, with her Gruumsbaggian hovering behind her. "Hi, Jack," she said, sounding miserable. Jack could not at first figure out why she was so upset at the presence of a Gruumsbaggian in the house, since the aliens had become ubiquitous in Jamesburg anyway.

He still did not understand when his mother walked with him through the living room, shadowed by her Gruumsbaggian, where they passed his father sitting in a chair reading a book.

Another Gruumsbaggian was leaning against the arm of the chair. It stared at Jack's mother as she passed by. "I'm not allowed to speak to your father," she said. "These Gruumsbaggians say we're divorced."

"That's right," Jack's father said. "If we speak to one another, or interact in any way, we'll be punished. These folks are here to make sure we behave." He indicated the Gruumsbaggians with a sweep of his hand. Both Gruumsbaggians tensed and looked at one another.

"Hey, I wasn't talking to her!" Jack's father said. "I was talking to my son. Divorced people are still allowed to talk to their children, you know!"

Jack groaned. He did not know that things would get even worse.

Chapter 9

The next morning Jack staggered, bleary-eyed and a little confused, with his father out towards where Railroad Avenue met the lake. They had at first been unsure of whether or not to report for the 'employment' that had been advertised in the newspapers, but they began to get ready to leave the house when the two Gruumsbaggians who were making sure Jack's mother and father stayed apart hinted that the men all needed to go to work, or they might be punished. And then four Gruumsbaggians in blue uniforms went through the neighborhood knocking on doors and confirming that any men who did not go to work would indeed be punished. As neither Jack nor his father had any great desire to be tarred and feathered, and it looked like they were going to have to find some way to get food as long as the Gruumsbaggians were prohibiting hunting and fishing anyway, they both ended up reporting for work that morning.

The Gruumsbaggians had not ordered any women to go to work. They had seen a lot of situation comedies from the 1950's and had other plans for them.

After The Blue

None of the humans tried to resist the Gruumsbaggians physically, except for Ghewen, who had run away. This was because the Gruumsbaggians were so much bigger and stronger than humans, because there were now so many of the aliens in and around Jamesburg, and because the humans all knew what the Gruumsbaggians had done a century earlier, even if the rumor was now circulating that it had been unintentional. And the people of Jamesburg did not know that every human life was so important to the Earth Project that the Gruumsbaggians were under orders not to kill any of them. Even the tar-like solution they used when they tarred and feathered people was non-toxic and harmless. But none of the humans knew that.

When Jack and his father got to the lake, they saw nearly the entire adult male population of Jamesburg, just under two thousand souls, gathered in the pale morning light. It was cool, and the black smoke was just as thick as it had been the day before. The men were unshaven and dressed sloppily, and they all coughed fitfully and shivered. They were sullen and cold. They looked like a bunch of robust, disgruntled prisoners of war, with Gruumsbaggians in blue uniforms as their guards.

Soon after Jack and his father arrived, buses began to drive up Railroad Avenue. Each of the buses was painted in bright swirls and pastels of exuberant color. Here and there, the chaotic patterns were adorned with little icons that looked either like old-time peace symbols, or perhaps Mercedes emblems, Jack wasn't sure which. A few of the buses even had slogans like 'I dig peace, man,' or 'You got to live free!' scrawled across their sides in whimsically drawn, brightly colored letters.

Russel Like

The buses were driven by Gruumsbaggians, and as each one came, the Gruumsbaggians in uniform would pick forty or fifty men out of the crowd and force them onto it. "Get on the buses to go to your jobs," the Gruumsbaggians would shout periodically. When each bus was full, its driver would throttle the engine and the bus would disappear down the other end of Railroad Avenue.

Finally Jack and his father were herded onto a bus. The seats were hard and cold and uncomfortable. "Well, son, this is it. I hope we're not making a mistake by letting them force us on this bus," Jack's father said. He was a slight, middle-aged man with an incipient paunch. He had two other, older children, a boy and a girl, who had both already married and been given their own houses by the council. Jack was the last child he had who was still living with him. Jack's father's specialty was marine biology. It was his job to guide and advise the fishing expeditions at the coast— among other things.

"Right. Me too," Jack said, in response to his father's comment. The bus lurched forward, and soon Jamesburg was behind them. Jack knew the road ended soon, as the people of Jamesburg had not maintained it for more than a few miles. He wondered what would happen when the bus came to the end of it.

***

More ships were streaming from the Gruumsbaggian Empire towards Earth. These ships did not carry humans, but rather buildings. More specifically, they carried strip malls—the kind of mall that was found along the road, separated from it by a parking lot, and which contained video stores, convenience stores, dry cleaners, and the like.

After The Blue

Here and there on Earth the Gruumsbaggians had been able to refurbish old strip malls, but in many places the original structures were just too decrepit to use. The strip malls were flimsier and had not weathered the last century as well as the big indoor malls, so on one of their colony planets the Gruumsbaggians had set up a vast factory to mass-produce strip malls. For they had realized something: there really wasn't much variety in the old strip malls. The factory could churn out thirty-seven identical strip malls per hour. Each one contained a convenience store, which was open around the clock, a dry-cleaner, a pizzeria, a video rental store, and an automatic teller machine. Occasionally, the factory used a custom-fitting operation, whereby one of the standard stores could be replaced by a hamburger restaurant or a billiards hall or an aerobics salon. But the customizing option wasn't used very often.

Of course, there still were not enough humans to go around. As it was, the Gruumsbaggians were having to spread their humans very thin. There were not nearly enough human teenagers to take over all the menial jobs in all the stores and businesses the Gruumsbaggians were opening. It was not a problem finding enough Gruumsbaggians to work in these menial positions, as the Gruumsbaggian Empire was fabulously wealthy and had more workers suited for menial jobs than it knew what to do with. But it would have been nice to have humans working in all of the 7-Elevens and pizzerias and laundromats from the outset, rather than waiting until the human population could grow into them. Human staff would have added verisimilitude to these establishments. But the shortage of humans meant the Gruumsbaggians would have to guide the humans that much longer before the Earth Project could be considered a success.

Russel Like

***

Jack soon learned he need not worry about the road ending. The bus had traveled down Railroad Avenue to its terminus, where, as far as Jack could remember, the gravel faded into mud. But there wasn't any mud. At the end of the gravel there was seamless asphalt. There was also a big green sign over the road that said: 'Welcome to the New Jersey Freepikeway. Speed Limit 100 miles per hour.'

As soon as the bus got onto the road it slowed down to a crawl. The New Jersey Freepikeway was as wide as the Raritan River in New Brunswick. It was the widest road Jack had ever seen, and it was full of bumper-to-bumper traffic. There were thousands of cars covering the road in both directions—each one driven by a Gruumsbaggian. Some of the Gruumsbaggian drivers had gotten out of their cars and were wandering around, or sitting on top on the hoods, or having four-armed fistfights with other Gruumsbaggian drivers who had exited their cars.

Soon the bus lurched to a complete stop. Jack groaned. "Traffic jam," he said, and slumped down in his seat. When, in the course of his historical studies he had read about traffic jams, they had been one of the things that made him wonder whether the world wasn't a better place after the Blue. It seemed to him like traffic jams were as close to hell as most fairly prosperous Americans had ever gotten on a regular basis.

"Traffic jam? What's that?" asked his father, who had never heard of them.

For three hours they sat in the traffic. Every now and then the traffic would clear up a little and the bus would lurch forward a

140

few hundred feet. Once the bus was able to travel uninterrupted for ten minutes before it came screeching to a halt in front of a group of Gruumsbaggians having a picnic on top of several stalled cars. Jack and his father and the other men from Jamesburg squirmed uncomfortably in their seats and wondered what exactly was going to happen to them. They spoke and muttered about it, but they were all too frightened to actually do anything. These were not a known quantity, like wild dogs or the wind and cold, that they would have to fight. These were Gruumsbaggians and they seemed as inscrutable as the deepest mysteries of the cosmos.

Finally, off to the right, they could see the New York City skyline in the distance. Sooty black clouds swirled around the tops of the skyscrapers, but still, the buildings were visible. Jack gasped, because it looked so different. He had seen the skyline before, and had even been to Manhattan. From the train terminal on Raritan Bay the people of Jamesburg had boats which they could use to visit the island, but for as long as Jack could remember, Manhattan had been a derelict wasteland of crumbling towers and rotting automobiles. Even from a distance, though, the difference was obvious. There were at least thirty or forty glittering new towers on the island. The Gruumsbaggians had rebuilt Manhattan. Soon the bus passed a sign that said: 'You are leaving the New Jersey Freepikeway. Have a nice drive.' Then it went onto a bridge over the Hudson River and into New York City.

***

Farnstarfl had noticed that there were a variety of cultures on Earth. He had also realized that one of them, the one that

141

involved fast food restaurants, and shopping malls, and superhighways, and televisions, and multinational corporations, and videocassette players, had been creeping into every corner of the world, especially during the few years right before the visit of the original Gruumsbaggian scouting team. So he had ordered these things to be placed all over the planet, even in places where there were other things, like pyramids or huts of mud and straw.

And thus was the globalization of world culture completed not by the financial moguls of Wall Street or the marketing geniuses of Madison Avenue, nor by the Hollywood elite, nor the rapacious successors of the robber barons, but by a race of four-armed, blue-haired, banana-yellow beings from a planet hundreds of light-years away.

***

The bus stopped on a street corner and the Gruumsbaggian driver stood up and turned to face the passengers, slouching so his head would not scrape the ceiling. "All right," he said, "this is where you all have to get out to go to your jobs. Come back here later to go home."

"When? When do we come back here?" Jack said.

"Good question," said his father. "Oh well. If nothing else, this should be interesting, don't you think?"

"Oh, of course. Loads of fun." Jack looked outside the bus. The buildings all seemed to be in good repair, unlike what he was accustomed to seeing in Manhattan. And, also unusual, the fully reconstructed sidewalks were packed—with Gruumsbaggians.

After The Blue

They were mostly dressed in suits and ties. Some of them were also wearing stovepipe hats, and some were wearing delicate black gloves on all four hands. They were pushing and shoving and falling all over one another on the sidewalk. The sidewalks had become a blur of yellow skin and blue hair and synthetic fabrics. The streets, too, were full of cars driven by Gruumsbaggians, like the ones that had blocked them on the New Jersey Freepikeway.

Several other Gruumsbaggians clambered onto the bus. "You have to get out now and go to work!" one of them shouted. "We have been authorized to punish anyone who doesn't go to work!"

Sullenly, the men began to file out of the bus. When Jack's father emerged into the gloomy, smoke-filled air, a Gruumsbaggian clutched at his wrist and said, "Come with me. I'll show you to your job." The men who had already exited the bus were all being led off by different Gruumsbaggians.

"Wait, what about my son?" Jack's father said.

"He has a different job. Come with me."

"I'll see you later, Jack!"

"Bye, Dad!" said Jack, who had been immediately behind his father. "Uh, have a good day, I guess!"

Then a Gruumsbaggian clutched at Jack's arm. "Come with me. I'll show you to your job," the alien said.

They had to fight their way through the throngs of Gruumsbaggians on the sidewalk. Sometimes, it seemed, huge yellow figures would just place themselves directly in front of them, actually attempting to get in their way. One Gruumsbaggian they passed was dressed in tattered old clothing. He held out a battered fedora to them and said, in the most plaintive voice a Gruumsbaggian could manage, "Won't you please write me a check for a cup of coffee? Won't you please write me a check?"

One group of Gruumsbaggians they passed was particularly striking. One of them wore big red floppy shoes, a curly red wig, sleeveless yellow overalls, red-and-white striped pants, and had his face painted snow-white. Another wore a billowing, bell-shaped garment of bluish fur. A third wore a black-and-white striped outfit with a cape. Over these outfits, each of them was doing his best to wear a suit and tie. Jack was so astonished at their appearance that for a moment he forgot his annoyance and frustration and stared at them. They passed by quickly, but before they did, Jack was sure he heard the one in the red wig say something about french fries and milkshakes.

The Gruumsbaggian who had Jack by the wrist was silent the whole way, except once, after they had traveled several blocks, when he said "We're almost there."

"Almost where?"

"Here," said the Gruumsbaggian, and towed Jack into the foyer of one of the skyscrapers. They they got into an elevator.

Jack knew what an elevator was. He'd seen them, but the ones he had seen were permanently stuck on the floors on which he had seen them. He had never been in a working elevator.

Nor had he ever before been in an elevator which contained an elevator operator. The operator of this elevator was, of course, a Gruumsbaggian, and when Jack and his escort entered, the operator said, "What floor?"

"Nine," answered the escort, and after the door was closed the elevator began to ascend. The Gruumsbaggian elevator operator clasped all four of his hands behind his back and made a noise which was supposed to approximate a clearing of the throat. "It is my pleasure to inform you," he said, "that as the operator of this elevator, I am empowered by the State with the authority to conduct marriages, preside over funerals, issue speeding tickets, Oh! Excuse me, we have arrived at your floor."

The door slid open and Jack's escort led him out and to an office suite. The Gruumsbaggian opened the door, thrust Jack inside and shouted, "Your employee is here!"

The door slammed shut behind him, and Jack found himself in what, for the twentieth century, would have been a fairly typical office, with desks and cubicles and industrial-style fluorescent lights and beige carpeting. Except that the office, like the city below it, was filled with Gruumsbaggians in various modes of attire. One of them, a particularly tall Gruumsbaggian in a navy blue suit, patent leather shoes, a wide red necktie, and a big black ten-gallon hat, came over to him.

"You're late!" the Gruumsbaggian said. "Very late! Do you think we can just function here without you? Do you? Why were you so late?"

"Why? Because...Because the bus, the traffic..."

The Gruumsbaggian cut him off with a wave of his lower right hand. "I don't want to hear it. Just don't let it happen again. And look at you!" shouted the Gruumsbaggian, pointing at Jack's plain wool sweater and wool slacks. "The way you're dressed! This is a professional organization! Do you want to ruin our reputation? Put on some proper clothes! Gertrude, give this man some clothes!"

A Gruumsbaggian in a pink dress got up from behind a typewriter, and, despite the high heels he was wearing, managed to avoid tipping over. "Here are your clothes," said Gertrude, handing Jack an orange suit, a mauve tie, a pair of yellow and green striped leather shoes, and a large furry hat with a chin strap. Jack recognized the hat as the kind he'd seen the guards at Windsor Castle wearing in old movies—busbys.

All of the Gruumsbaggians who came to Earth to work on the Earth Project were male, but it did not bother the male Gruumsbaggian in the 'Gertrude' position at all to be wearing a dress and high heels, which were, of course, designed to fit his seven-and-a-half foot, four-armed physique. To him, wearing the outfit was just a part of his job. The dress and the shoes were props, costumes, nothing more. And anyway, human conventions regarding gender and dress were meaningless to Gruumsbaggians.

"Now put all of that on," said the other Gruumsbaggian, who was obviously supposed to be Jack's boss, "and don't let me see you without any of it again. We have a professional image to uphold! And get right to work. You think we can manage with you gone half the day? Gertrude, please show him to his workstation after he has changed."

Jack wasn't going to put the clothing on, but Gertrude insisted on watching him until he did, so, reluctantly, he put on the slacks and jacket and shirt and tie and busby. He was not accustomed to dressing that way. In Jamesburg no one ever told anyone else how to dress, and he found it very uncomfortable. The shoes cut into his heels, the jacket restricted his arms from moving, and the tie felt choking. The busby was particularly stifling. It was very heavy and his head began to drip with sweat almost from the moment he put it on.

After The Blue

"Okay," said Gertrude, when Jack was finished changing, "follow me." The Gruumsbaggian led Jack to a tiny cubicle away from any windows and told him to sit down at the chair that was positioned at the desk there. "Now get to work."

Jack sat and looked at the things arrayed on his desk. As he looked down, the busby nearly tumbled off of his head. He almost tightened the chin strap, but then glanced around quickly to make sure he was not being watched, took it off, and hid it underneath his chair. Then he tore off the tie and put it with the hat.

On his desk was a box of paper clips, a stapler, a pair of scissors, an unsharpened pencil, some tweezers, a blank sheet of paper, and an eyedropper filled with whiteout. He wondered what he was supposed to do with all of it.

As he sat there, uncertain about what to do next, he realized Gruumsbaggians were passing by every few minutes. Finally he said to one of them, "Excuse me, can you tell me what to do with all of this?"

The Gruumsbaggian stopped and scratched his head with his lower left and upper right arms. "Hmmm, Let's see. No, I really don't know," he said. "Let me get Captain Phillips."

Captain Phillips was apparently the Gruumsbaggian who had yelled at him when he arrived, and was apparently the boss, because that Gruumsbaggian came running over to Jack's cubicle a moment later.

"What? What is this? You're not wearing your hat?" exclaimed the Gruumsbaggian from underneath his big ten-gallon hat. "Or your tie? Put them back on immediately. Now."

"But they're not helping me to do my work at all. There's no reason..."

"That doesn't matter. They show you're a professional. What if someone comes in here who's not from our office and sees you sitting there without them? Then they'll believe you're the janitor. Put them back on. You're lucky enough to have professional-caliber work, where you have a lot of autonomy. You should be grateful."

"But..."

"If you don't put them back on we're going to have to have you punished."

"All right, all right," Jack said, reluctantly putting the tie and the busby back on. This time, though, he kept the tie and the chin strap a little looser.

"Now what was this about your work?" demanded Captain Phillips.

"Uh, yes. My work. What exactly am I supposed to be doing with these things?"

The Gruumsbaggian stared at him for a moment with what Jack guessed was supposed to be barely concealed anger. "I shouldn't have to tell you that," he finally said. "You are in a professional-level position. You should know by now what your job is. Everything you need is right here. And remember, we're counting on you." Then he walked away.

The Gruumsbaggian had not told Jack what he was supposed to do largely because the Gruumsbaggians had simply been completely unable to figure out what it was that went on in offices. From their viewing of videotapes, they had gleaned a fairly good idea of what offices looked like, and of which implements were to be found

After The Blue

in them, but the actual workings of offices were as inscrutable to them as the rules to Monopoly or the purposes of rides at amusement parks.

They had hoped that if the humans were put in offices with all of the right items, they would know, intrinsically, what to do. After all, the Gruumsbaggians knew that when they put a Gruumsbaggian lornquat tree snake in a lornquat tree, it always found food, and when they put a Gruumsbaggian pigdog in a forest, it would never starve because it would always know where to find fungus.

***

Sheila had returned to the McDonald's. She had originally decided to stay in Jamesburg, but after the morning's events she concluded she was better off, at least for the time being, with Fred.

For after the men had all been sent off on the buses, a Gruumsbaggian had been assigned to each woman in Jamesburg. The Gruumsbaggian assigned to Sheila hadn't known she already had a job, and so treated her just like the other women in town. He had taken her into the kitchen of the house in Jamesburg which the council had given to her and ordered her to bake cookies. She was accustomed to listening to Gruumsbaggians, so at first she did what she was told. She mixed the batter, preheated the oven, formed the batter into little drops, and placed them on the cookie sheet the Gruumsbaggian had provided.

And after they had begun to cook and the aroma of chocolate chips had begun to waft throughout the house, she asked what she was supposed to do next.

"Start preparing more cookies," the Gruumsbaggian told her.

"And what am I supposed to do after that?" she said.

"Bake more cookies."

When she heard this, she began to wonder. She remembered everything Jack had told her, and how Jack and the other people of Jamesburg seemed upset at what the Gruumsbaggians had done so recently to all of the trees, and the air, and the lake. It was then that she passed a critical point, the point at which her allegiance shifted irrevocably from the side of the Gruumsbaggians to the side of the humans of Jamesburg. It was then that she decided she was not going to spend her day baking one tray of chocolate chip cookies after another.

"You know, I work in McDonald's," she said.

"You do?" said the Gruumsbaggian. He seemed surprised.

"Yes. And I have to get back to work."

The Gruumsbaggian promptly let her go, and she began making her way back to Fred and the restaurant. Even if she had decided no longer to trust the Gruumsbaggians in general, she still liked Fred, and working in the McDonald's seemed preferable to what she was doing in Jamesburg.

She made her way through a town suffused with the mingled odors of baking chocolate chip cookies from a thousand ovens and foul black smoke.

***

At his office in New York City, Jack was idly playing with the paper clips and thinking. He had made a long chain of about thirty paper clips and was jangling it back and forth. That, and stapling the sheet of paper folded over itself, were his only material achievements of the day so far.

But he was thinking very hard about the book he was writing with the help of some of the councilors. He was thinking about it particularly hard as it seemed like the only way out of his current situation. He pined longingly for the days before the return of the Gruumsbaggians, when everything seemed to make sense, and life had at least not been unpleasant.

The book was not finished yet, but it had been started. It had a cover page that listed a copyright of 1976. That was important. It was critical that the Gruumsbaggians believe the book to have been written *before* the Blue. That cover page had been copied from another book they had, one that actually had been printed in 1976. The text of the book began like this:

INTRODUCTION

It is odd that the curious town of Jamesburg has received so little attention from sociologists, anthropologists, and the press, because Jamesburg and its 'Plain People,' as they call themselves, are increasingly unusual in our rapidly industrializing world. Jamesburg has existed for centuries amidst the hubbub and tumult of New Jersey's increasingly urbanized landscape. While superhighways, factories, and massive office buildings have covered nearly every section of New Jersey in recent years, the town of Jamesburg remains a place strangely apart.

151

Russel Like

The people who live there coexist with the larger society but do not have much to do with it. In this book we will attempt to describe some of the quali- ties that make Jamesburg so unique in our modern world.

Some more had been written, but not nearly enough. As the time dragged on, Jack could not wait until he would be allowed to leave to work on the book.

Chapter 10

A few miles away from Jamesburg, Henry and Desmond Ghewen were sitting in a small thicket of trees the Gruumsbaggians had not cut down. Henry had managed to find Ghewen without too much trouble. Ghewen had been wandering furtively around the outskirts of the buildings the Gruumsbaggians had erected around Jamesburg. Under the cover of darkness, Henry had simply wandered around, yelling "Desmond! Desmond Ghewen!" This had not seemed to bother the Gruumsbaggians, but it bothered Ghewen, who was trying to stay hidden, and he crept over to find out who was shouting his name. Then he approached Henry from behind, grabbed him, put a hand over his mouth, made him lie down behind some tree stumps, and said, "Henry! What are you trying to do? Don't you know they think I'm a criminal? Please, please be quiet!"

***

Russel Like

Ghewen did not know it, of course, but his escape had been permitted. In fact, it had been the source of much joy at the local Gruumsbaggian Earth Project Control Center. For now, the Gruumsbaggians felt they were truly beginning to succeed in their endeavor. In Ghewen, they had created a fugitive from justice, and they knew there had been plenty of those on pre-epidemic Earth.

So all of the Gruumsbaggian authorities were under orders to pretend to want to catch Ghewen but to actually leave him alone. For a time.

***

"So here we are, both fugitives from the Gruumsbaggians," Ghewen said. "I don't know about you, but I'm not willing to be tarred and feathered. I've had just about enough of them and their ridiculous shenanigans and I'm not going to take it anymore. By the way, did you hear anything about Jenny today? I want to speak to her, but I'm hesitant to go back into town." Jenny was Ghewen's wife.

"Yeah, I did," Henry said. "The Gruumsbaggians went over to her and told her she'd have to be a prostitute. Last I saw, she was being guarded by one of them and standing out on a street corner in a really short skirt."

A storm of anger raged across Ghewen's face. "That's it," he growled. "That's the last straw. They're going to pay!"

Henry knew how Ghewen felt. He felt pretty much the same way himself and was glad to have an ally. He had been fuming ever since they told him he would have to be a homosexual. It was almost like they were making fun of him for being given such poor

154

choices for marriage. He was still somewhat bitter about that. And now it seemed like Ghewen might even be receptive to an idea he had, an idea that sounded like a lot of fun. "Jack was telling me," he began, slowly and carefully, "that one of the stores the Gruumsbaggians put up sells weapons, all sorts of weapons."

***

Now that steps had been taken to recreate such crucial elements of human society as pollution, traffic, and corporate offices, Farnstarfl was able to turn his attention to other, more esoteric, matters. He was engaging in a period of academic relaxation, and he was taking some time to think about whatever caught his fancy. There were many minor things about Earth and humans that had been bothering him. For example, he had learned that the leaves of many Earth trees turned brown and gold and red and fell off each year. And he had also learned that the hair of many human men fell out and did not grow back. And he knew, also, that all life on Earth was based on DNA and seemed to be descended from a common ancestor.

But what he could not understand was why humans and trees weren't more similar. Why didn't the hair of human men, instead of falling out, turn brilliant hues of red and orange and gold each autumn and then fall out, only to be replaced by tender green shoots of hair the following spring? Or, conversely, why didn't the leaves of trees, instead of falling out every year, just turn gray or white late in the tree's life, and fall off entirely and not grow back? He had interrogated Harold and Ferdinand, the two human historians, on this point, but they had been of little help.

155

It was matters like these that occupied Farnstarfl for several days while he took a break from the weightier matters involving the Earth Project.

Even though he was taking a break, he considered, from time to time, some slightly more serious matters. He wondered whether they had put advertisements on enough animals. They had put advertisements on fish, and on deer, and on some rabbits, but that had been about it. The technical part of getting the advertisements on—that is, the manipulation of the living tissue—was easy. It was child's play for Gruumsbaggian science. What was difficult was to decide whether or not to begin placing advertisements on the sides of whales, for instance. Farnstarfl was having an awfully hard time trying to figure out whether the pre-epidemic humans would have put advertisements on whales. In fact he had not found any direct evidence that they put advertisements on any animals at all. Then again, he hadn't found any direct evidence that they had *not* put advertisements on animals. He knew that just because he hadn't found any records of it didn't mean it hadn't happened. He was simply extrapolating.

But he didn't fret about it too much. The beer and cigarette advertisements on the sides of whales could wait a few days.

***

Henry and Ghewen, the gangling red-haired teenager and the powerful bronze adult, had ventured out of their thicket and were taking a walk in a direction away from Jamesburg. They felt safe, in part because vast rolling clouds of thick, black smoke had

156

begun to engulf their area and visibility was very low. It was impossible to tell whether the smoke was coming from the machine near Lake Manalapan or not; it was sufficient that it helped to hide them. And Ghewen wanted to do some more exploring of the area while they had some cover.

Henry was feeling quite happy for the first time in quite a while. When he suggested that they loot a Gruumsbaggian weapons shop, Ghewen agreed immediately. Henry was surprised, because he had a nagging suspicion that his suggestion to begin blowing things up might be regarded as childish, but when Ghewen, an adult whom he knew to be regarded as intelligent, responsible, and mature, and who had been one of his schoolteachers, welcomed his suggestion, his fears evaporated. Then Henry thought that perhaps he wasn't being so childish after all. He did not consider that exceptional circumstances could make even the most stable people act with reckless abandon.

"Anyway, Henry," Ghewen said as they left the thicket and began walking down a road the Gruumsbaggians had apparently built, "I just want to see what they've done around here. We'll try to keep hidden, but I'm not sure if they'll be after me or not. If I've come to any conclusions about the Gruumsbaggians, it's this: they often make very little sense, at least to us."

"Yeah," Henry said. "So we'll go back to that weapons shop Jack told me about?"

"Well, let's not rush into any decisions, yet. I just want to see what they've done around here first. Now let's see, what used to be here? Some woods and maybe a couple of cornfields? Is that right?"

"And a mud road."

They did not see any more woods, or any cornfields, or a mud road. The asphalt they were walking on had begun near the little thicket and after traversing an area of stumps for a few minutes, it was bordered on either side by sprawling, one-story houses with driveways and large front yards. The front yards had lush lawns of thick green grass perhaps an inch high, and were adorned with shrubs and flowers. There were cars in many of the driveways. "These are the kind of houses they built right before the catastrophe," Ghewen said. "I wonder who the Gruumsbaggians are building them for?"

Just then the front door of one of the houses burst open and a Gruumsbaggian emerged. He was wearing blue shorts and a white T-shirt that said 'Perot in 2000.' By his lower left hand he led a small human child. The Gruumsbaggian did not seem to pay any attention to Henry or Ghewen. Instead, he led the child over to the garage, which he opened, and then said to the child, "Now we're going to mow the lawn." He rolled a lawn mower out of the garage and started it up. No sooner had he started, though, than a Gruumsbaggian came running out of a neighboring house and waved all of his arms at him as if trying to tell him something. The first Gruumsbaggian shut the mower off.

"You're not supposed to mow the lawn today," said the second Gruumsbaggian. "It's not Saturday."

"Oh? Well, I can mow the lawn whenever I want."

"No you can't. It says, if you look, on Page 437 of the *Suburban Guidelines*, that mowing is done only on Saturdays."

"You'll have to show me."

"Fine, I will, if you're not going to do your job and teach this human how to live properly."

After The Blue

Henry and Ghewen exchanged glances of disbelief. Then they kept walking, and the sounds of the two Gruumsbaggians arguing faded in the distance behind them.

***

When Captain Phillips told Jack that he would have to report to a meeting, he had at first been overjoyed. The cubicle was dim and joyless, and sitting there staring at his paper clips and staples, he felt himself to be going slowly insane. He thought anything had to be better than that.

But the meeting was really not much better. Captain Phillips, after ordering him to straighten his tie and tighten the chin strap on his busby, had directed Jack to a small, square, windowless room with an L-shaped table. Already seated there were seven or eight Gruumsbaggians. Captain Phillips told Jack to sit in one of the empty chairs and then seated himself at a big chair at the end of the table.

After sitting in complete silence for about ten minutes, Jack began to wonder what the meeting was about. "Um...what is this meeting for, anyway?" he asked.

"Shhh!" Captain Phillips hissed at him angrily. "We're having a meeting! Don't interrupt!"

Jack waited through another silent twenty minutes, during which they all sat there staring blankly at one another until he spoke again. "So when are we going to start?" he said.

Captain Phillips glared at him again. "If you continue interrupting we'll never get finished. Now please keep quiet for the rest of the meeting."

The Gruumsbaggians knew meetings had been a part of business life on pre-epidemic Earth. And they had read the definition of 'meeting' in a copy of Webster's New Collegiate Dictionary. The definition said a meeting was 'an assembly for a common purpose.' It said nothing about discussion.

The meeting lasted an hour and a half.

By the end of the meeting Jack was feeling sick. He had not eaten anything since the morning, but he felt a need to sit down in the bathroom for a while. He wondered if the cause were perhaps the stress of being at the Gruumsbaggian workplace, or the horrible black stuff that he had been forced to breathe in lately, or just a virus. He asked Gertrude for directions to the bathroom. Once there, he shut himself in the stall and felt almost grateful for the privacy from the Gruumsbaggians.

He had wrenching diarrhea but afterwards felt much better. He was sitting on the toilet for a minute, regaining his composure, when someone began to knock energetically on the door of his stall. "What is it?"

"It's Captain Phillips. I want to know why you're taking so long. There's work to be done!"

Jack groaned. "I'm not feeling well. There's nothing I could do about it! What did you want me to do?"

"I'm not sure you have a valid reason for being in there. I think you may just be slacking off." Then the stall began to shake, and, with a loud crunching sound, the stall door came off. Jack looked up to see Captain Phillips grasping the door in all four hands. "Now I want you to get back to work as soon as possible," the Gruumsbaggian said sternly. "Is that clear?"

After The Blue

If Jack had not already become accustomed to having absurdity piled upon absurdity, he might have been incredulous. As it was, he was not even embarrassed. He was simply further annoyed and his resolve to finish the book that would make the Gruumsbaggians leave them alone was strengthened. But he did not want to be tarred and feathered or worse. "Okay, I'll be done in a second." he said. "Um...could you put the door back though?"

Captain Phillips, after a few moments scrutinizing Jack, leaned the stall door back against one of the side walls of the stall so that Jack was half-concealed. Then the Gruumsbaggian called out, as if there were a completely functional stall door between himself and Jack and they could no longer see one another's faces, "Now get back to work as soon as you can. We're not paying you to just sit in the bathroom all day, you know!"

***

The first chapter of the book Jack was helping to write and for which he was acting as historical consultant, the book that was supposed to deceive the Gruumsbaggians into leaving the people of Jamesburg alone, was about the economy of Jamesburg. "The people of Jamesburg," it began, "have little commerce with the rest of the world.

"For as long as records have been kept," it continued, "the Plain People have grown or hunted their own food. The farmland in the surrounding area is sufficiently productive to feed the entire population when combined with the deer they hunt and the fish and other creatures they catch in the lake

161

and in the ocean, to which they have a rail connection.

"The people of Jamesburg do have some slight trade with the outside world. Their agricultural operations are so efficient that they can occasionally trade surplus crops for manufactured goods such as automobiles or electronics. So thrifty are the legendary Plain People of Jamesburg, though, that any such goods which they purchase are repaired for as long as possible and are almost never discarded."

***

Henry and Ghewen passed a number of houses. Sometimes there were Gruumsbaggians outside, mowing or doing other yard work. As it became apparent that none of them had any desire to arrest Ghewen, the two humans stopped trying to hide behind clouds of smoke or shrubs or whatever else was convenient. At a number of the houses they saw little human children. The children, when they saw the two humans from Jamesburg, generally seemed to shrink back behind the protection of the Gruumsbaggians. This prompted Ghewen to speak.

"Give them to me before they're seven and they're mine for life," he muttered.

"What?" Henry said.

"Oh, nothing. It's just—well, first of all, I wonder where they got all of these children. Must have had something to do with the wanderers and why there aren't any more. But think about it!

You've seen what these Gruumsbaggians are doing! And now they're going to raise these kids here! How do you think these kids are going to turn out when they're grown up?"

Henry gulped. "Oh boy," he said.

"And it looks like there will be a lot more of them than there are of us. We've got to do something," Ghewen said. "Where's that weapons shop?"

It turned out there was no need for them to go back to the weapons shop in Jamesburg, for soon the houses gave way to a strip of free-standing stores, including a McDonald's, twenty-five other fast food restaurants, seventy-three shoe stores, forty-four clothing stores, and a store named 'Crazy Joe's Rifle and Gun Shoppe.' They walked in and looked around. There was just one Gruumsbaggian, who stood behind a counter in the store. The merchandise was similar to what Jack said he had seen in the other weapons shop. There were rifles, pistols, submachine guns, hand grenades, and bazookas.

"Ah yes," Ghewen said, smiling guilefully, "I have read several books about the old weapons. They seem to have done a good job of making things that resemble them here. They must think all of these things were just sold on every street corner. Come over here with me."

He stepped over to the counter. "I'm interested in making a purchase," he said to the proprietor, "but first I'd like to try some of these out."

"Why, certainly," answered the Gruumsbaggian. He gestured with all four arms. "Which one would you like to try?"

Ghewen pointed to a small semiautomatic rifle. "That one," he said. "And make sure to give me the ammunition."

The Gruumsbaggian obediently gave Ghewen all of the material. "Here you are, sir,"

"Thank you very much," Ghewen replied. He carefully loaded the gun. Then he pointed it at the Gruumsbaggian, pulled the trigger, and blew his brains out.

The Gruumsbaggians in the area had actually all been given orders to let Ghewen do just about whatever he wanted. He was a fugitive, an authentic fugitive from justice who had run away from them, and he represented one of their greatest successes to date in the Earth Project. They were not about to ruin one of their successes in restoring Earth to its former status by capturing him. That was, in part, why the proprietor had been so cooperative. Of course, he had also been so cooperative because he wasn't very bright, having been shipped out to work on the Earth Project only after being unemployed for many years because he was not intelligent enough to handle any real Gruumsbaggian job.

The Gruumsbaggian bled purple blood and quickly expired. His was the first Gruumsbaggian death ever caused by a human. But it would not be the last.

***

Feeling better since relieving himself, Jack was beginning to get very hungry. He was at first hesitant to inquire about the subject of food, for fear of the kind of response he would get. But finally his hunger prevailed and he asked Captain Phillips if he could perhaps have something to eat. Surprisingly, Captain Phillips' response was almost jovial. "Oh yes! To celebrate your first day, I will be taking you out! Come on, let's go!"

As happy as he was at the prospect of getting some food, Jack was not sure whether to expect a lunch provided by the Gruumsbaggian to be at all nourishing, or filling, or whether he would actually get any food at all. Jack and the Gruumsbaggian boarded the elevator where the operator continued to talk about presiding over marriages and issuing speeding tickets. They disembarked on the ground floor and went out into the street.

The street was just as crowded with Gruumsbaggians as it had been earlier in the day. Across the street, Jack was able to glimpse Allan Barnes, one of the men from Jamesburg, being led somewhere by a Gruumsbaggian, but was unable to shout across the sea of yellow aliens. He knew there had to be other men from Jamesburg sprinkled throughout the Gruumsbaggians thronging the sidewalks, but he could not see any.

The lunch, while it filled him up, was anything but pleasant. They went to a restaurant nearby, which, Jack noticed, didn't serve any animal cuisine but instead was called 'John Smith's American Restaurant.' After they were seated by the Gruumsbaggian maitre'd and given menus, Jack began to think and hope, for the first time, that he might actually have a pleasant experience.

Then a Gruumsbaggian came over to the table and asked if he could take their orders. Jack was eyeing the fried chicken on the menu, but Captain Phillips spoke before he could say anything. "Yes," he said. "I will have the hamburger, and my associate here will have...let me see..." He produced a small chart. Then he said to Jack, "What have you had to eat today?"

"Uh...just some toast and milk..."

"Oh. Well, I see from this nutritional chart that you'll have to have, let me see, a plate of brussels sprouts, a broiled liver, and

165

a glass of orange juice. There." He handed the waiter both of their menus. "And take your elbows off of the table," he said to Jack.

Jack began to feel sick again.

***

Ghewen and Henry were busily loading up a station wagon with rifles, submachine guns, hand grenades, hand-held flame-throwers, and large quantities of ammunition. "These Gruumsbag-gians must really have thought this was a violent society," Ghewen said. "It will be my pleasure to prove them right."

They had taken the station wagon, at gunpoint, from a Gruumsbaggian who had stopped at a neighboring store. It was the first carjacking on Earth in nearly a hundred years. Farnstarfl was very excited when he heard about it.

Henry began inspecting some of the weapons. He picked up a semiautomatic, pointed it idly across the street, and peered through the sights.

"I'd be delighted to show you how to work these things, Henry," Ghewen said. "The Gruumsbaggians seem to have designed these for ease of use. Now, about this semiautomatic. You take the ammunition clip and you put it here..."

***

By the time they returned to the office from lunch, the clock on the wall said 4:03. Jack knew that conventional working hours, in the world before the Blue, used to end at five. He began figuring out how many seconds it would be until the end of the day when a

166

necessary part of the book they were writing occurred to him. He unstapled the piece of paper on his desk, grabbed a pencil, and began to write.

"The Plain People of Jamesburg," he wrote, "appear to be strangely immune to most of the diseases that affect other humans. Medical experts are not sure why this is so. Some say it is because the Plain People generally marry only other Plain People, and there is something in their common genetic background that protects them from most human diseases. Others speculate that it may be their diet, or their manner of living, or perhaps something in the soil in which they grow their crops. Whatever the real reason, the Plain People of Jamesburg remain largely unaffected by epidemics that sweep through the larger society."

Jack put down his pencil and read over what he had written. It seemed clear enough. He folded up the piece of paper, stuck it in his pocket, and glanced at the clock. It said 4:10. At five o'clock, he decided, he would tell them he was leaving. He shuffled his feet idly beneath his desk. He felt bored, trapped, and isolated, and there was no reason for him to stay. He could not wait to go.

***

"Now," Ghewen said, "it's time for a gesture. A minor action. Something that will convey our true feelings about the whole state of affairs."

"Yeah!" Henry said. "It's time to blow something up!"

Ghewen smiled. "Exactly." He peered down the highway and pointed at a strip mall some distance away. "You see that little place down there? About five hundred feet down on the right? Next to the smoke cloud? It's called the New Jersey Stores." Henry nodded. "Get in the station wagon. That's where we're going."

***

When the clock reached 4:45, Jack unstrapped his busby and set it beneath his chair. He removed his tie and jacket and put on the clothes he had worn in the morning. Then Captain Phillips came by.

"What? I was just coming by to see how you were doing with your work, and you're getting ready to leave? We still have some very important work to do! Now put your hat and your tie back on and sit back down!"

"But it's almost five o'clock! Isn't it time to go?"

The Gruumsbaggian sat down on the floor and leaned his head forward, as if he were being conspiratorial. "Look," he said, "you can't stay just until five o'clock. Not if you ever want to get anywhere in this organization. You'll have to work much harder than that. You understand, don't you?"

"Well, that's all right," Jack said. "I don't think I really want to get anywhere in this organization, to tell you the truth. So I'll just go now anyway."

Captain Phillips held up his upper right hand. "No, I'm sorry. I can't allow you to go yet. We have some very important work coming up, and I'll need your help."

"Oh. I see. More important than what I've been working on all day?"

"Much more," said the Gruumsbaggian, apparently ignoring, or not getting, Jack's sarcasm. "I'll tell you when you can

168

leave. And another thing. I don't think you really appreciate this job. In this job you don't have to get yourself dirty, and you get to use your mind. You have a lot of autonomy but you just don't seem to appreciate it. Now my advice to you is to get a better attitude. I don't know if this means anything to you, but in two weeks you'll get paid. Then you'll be able to afford all of those things you see in the mall, like those plastic ducks that dunk their beaks in the water. If nothing else helps your attitude, maybe when you think about that, you'll realize this is all worth it. You'll remember what you're working for."

***

The 'New Jersey Stores' contained a pizzeria, a dry- cleaning establishment, a videocassette rental store, a billiards hall, and a convenience store. "Okay, are we all set?" Ghewen said. "Hand grenades, flamethrowers, and semiautomatics? Anything else?"

Henry scanned the mall. He saw Gruumsbaggian proprietors in all of them when something caught his eye. "There!" he said. "There's a human in that videocassette store!"

"There is? Come on, let's take a look before we do anything."

They went inside. The human, a young man about Henry's age, seemed genuinely shocked to see them. He stared at Ghewen. "Are...are you an adult?" he stammered. The fact that Henry and Ghewen were armed to the teeth, with hand grenades in belts and bandoleers slung across their chests, did not seem to concern him.

"Yes I am, young man. Do you know a girl named Sheila?"

"Yes, I do. Why? Have you seen her?"

169

"Yes I have. And I think there's a lot I can teach you." Ghewen put a massive arm protectively around the young man's shoulder. "What's your name, son?"

"Bob."

Ghewen continued, "Well, Bob, I think you'd better come outside with us, because we're about to blow this building up. And after that I'll tell you some stories about Gruumsbaggians that will make your head spin."

***

Jack stared miserably at the clock, which now read 5:45. Sweat was dripping from his head because a whole day spent wearing the busby had made him very hot. Then his Gruumsbaggian boss came over, holding a piece of paper. He handed the paper to Jack.

"Here's the work I needed you for," he said "We need one photocopy of that. Do you know where the photocopier is? It's right over there." He pointed.

Jack looked the paper. It was blank on one side. On the other side it said 'Memo.' That was all. "I can leave after I copy this?" he said.

"If you must."

Within five minutes Jack was out of the office, trying to remember the way back to the bus stop and pushing and shoving through throngs of yellow flesh. He was thankful to be out of the office, of course, but he was haunted by Captain Phillips' parting words, words which reverberated down the corners of his skull and made him despair for the future.

The words had been "See you tomorrow."

***

"Now, Bob," Ghewen said, "I want you to watch us carefully. I know you were raised on Gruums-Baag, but now I'm going to begin teaching you how humans on Earth really live. Okay, Henry. Go!"

The two let fly with a volley of hand grenades, followed by blasts of flamethrowers and a hail of semiautomatic fire. The mall turned into a panorama of collapsing roofs and imploding walls. Flaming shards of wood and plastic began to rain down for hundreds of feet around them. Several Gruumsbaggians ran out even as tongues of flame began to lick out and engulf the New Jersey Stores.

***

When Jack finally found the bus stop, after fighting his way through hordes of pushing, shoving Gruumsbaggians, one bus was full and was starting to pull away. There was another bus that was about half full. He couldn't find his father, and assuming he would be on another bus, found a seat in the front. Soon after Jack sat down, he saw a tarred and feathered human figure board the bus. The figure, which walked awkwardly, as if in great discomfort, plopped down in the seat next to him and groaned.

Jack peered at the figure's blackened face, which was relatively free of feathers. "Robert?" he said. "Robert Rosenthal? Is that you?"

"Yes, it is. Ow!" He put his hand up to his mouth. "Hurts to talk."

"Just please tell me one thing. What did you do to deserve this?"

171

"Wouldn't listen to boss. Tried to make me...eat vegetables..."

"Sorry," Jack said. "I won't make you talk any more. But I think that stuff comes off eventually." Jack shuddered. It didn't look like a whole lot of fun.

He looked under his seat where he found a newspaper. *The New York Times* was the name of the paper. The style looked similar to that of old copies of the *Times* he had seen on microfilm. He picked it up and read the headlines.

"New Revelations About Assassination of John F. Kennedy," read one. "Elvis Sighted in California Bodega," read another.

Soon the bus filled up with men from Jamesburg and left for New Jersey. It got dark on the way home, and since the bus had no lights, Jack had to stop reading the newspaper, which he had found to be mostly about John F. Kennedy and Elvis Presley.

***

Farnstarfl was ecstatic when he learned there was an authentic insurgency on Earth. He had gathered through his research that pre-epidemic Earth had been a somewhat violent place, and he took the spontaneous eruption of violence as a vindication of everything he had done so far. It meant things were going well with the Earth Project. Just to make sure, he asked the two captive Earth historians about this. "Was there much violence on Earth in the past?" he said, after summoning them to his office.

The two humans looked at one another. Then the older one, Ferdinand, answered. "Oh, yes. Very much. There were rebellions

172

all over the place, all the time. You'll see if you read about the end of the Soviet Union, or Yugoslavia, or if you read about the history of almost any country in the world. It was a very violent place."

"Very violent," Harold agreed.

Farnstarfl sent them back to their quarters, immensely satisfied with himself. He did not know that the two historians had prepared themselves for just such a moment. They had agreed that the people of Jamesburg might at some time begin to fight back and if they did, then the way to back them up was to convince Farnstarfl that things like this went on all the time.

**

When the bus had driven the forty miles back to Jamesburg—it had taken three hours again because of all the Gruumsbaggians and their cars on the road—Jack and the other men clambered eagerly off the bus. In the distance they heard faint cries of "You put your left foot in, you put your left foot out, you put your left foot in and you shake it all about..."

As Jack stepped off the bus and onto the pavement, a Gruumsbaggian grasped him by the shoulder and pulled him several dozen yards away. There several other men who had just gotten off of the bus had been forced to stand in a crude semicircle. The Gruumsbaggian made Jack join the semicircle. "Stay there!" the Gruumsbaggian ordered him. Within a few minutes, all of the men from the bus had joined them, and the humans formed a complete circle.

"Okay," said one of the Gruumsbaggians gaily, taking a position in the center of the circle, "it's time to unwind after a hard day's work at the office!" The Gruumsbaggian was clad in sweat pants and a plain orange T-shirt. "Let me show you how! First, you put your left leg in, like this!" The Gruumsbaggian kicked up his left leg. "Then you take it out! Then you do the hokey-pokey and you shake it all about!"

After the Gruumsbaggian had finished shaking his left leg all about, he said, "Now you try it!" When none of the men responded, the Gruumsbaggian in the center said, "Oh, come on! You don't want to be punished over this, do you?"

Sullenly, the men began to mouth the words and move their legs. "Come on, with more enthusiasm!" the Gruumsbaggian urged them. "Feel the burn! Feel the burn!"

Apparently the Gruumsbaggians expected them to do the hokey-pokey in a big circle next to the lake every day when they came home from work. "You have to have some fun when you come home!" the Gruumsbaggians told them as they danced. "Some activity to help you unwind from a hard day's work! It's very important for your mental well-being!"

Jack and the other men on his bus had to do the hokey-pokey for half an hour. It seemed especially difficult for those of them who had been tarred and feathered.

Chapter 11

For the most part, the Gruumsbaggians stood around in menacing little clumps while the men did the hokey-pokey. Occasionally, when one of the men seemed less than enthusiastic, a Gruumsbaggian would leave his clump, amble over, and say something like, "You're not putting your left foot in enough" or "you should try to sing louder." When Ted Archer, one of the men of Jamesburg, left the circle and sat down, exhausted, on the ground away from the rest of the men, two Gruumsbaggians rushed over, picked him up and took him away. During the moment of silence after he shouted "You put your left foot in" and before he shouted "you take your left foot out," Jack could hear the Gruumsbaggians telling Ted how he would be punished for refusing to unwind.

Finally one of the Gruumsbaggians announced, "Okay. You all seem sufficiently relaxed. You can go now." Grumbling and sweating, the men streamed back to their homes. When Jack's group cleared the site, the Gruumsbaggians had more men waiting to do the hokey-pokey. The Gruumsbaggians were having the men do the hokey-pokey in shifts.

Jack, though he was enervated from a long day spent sitting in the chair in the office and on the bus, and was tired from doing the hokey-pokey, hurried off to work on the book. He felt, even more than before, the urgency of his task. He kept remembering Captain Phillips' ominous words—"See you tomorrow"—and then he thought of the ludicrous traffic, and a half an hour of 'you put your left foot in' and so on at the end of the day, and of being made to wear that hot, uncomfortable, and totally unnecessary busby, and the rest of the outfit, just so he could sit in a chair and stare into space.

But before he could get to work on the book, he was intercepted by Sheila. "Please, Jack," she said, over the faint sounds of 'you put your right foot in' which came to them in the distance, "can you please finish telling me the history of Jamesburg now? I need to know it. I have to know it. The Gruumsbaggians—do you know what they were making everyone do here today?"

"No, but I know what they were making me do all day. And it was absurd." Jack said.

"They were making us bake cookies. And more cookies. And more cookies. It was so unbearable, I went back to the McDonald's. I don't know...it just seems like if I knew what happened, what really happened in the past, then maybe I'd be able to deal with the present a little better. So can you please finish telling me?"

Once again, Jack was unable to resist. He couldn't deny her, not when she looked at him so imploringly with her bright green eyes. He felt the crushing urgency of the need to work on the book, but decided he could spare at least a few minutes to tell her the rest of the story, even if he had to make it a little shorter than it perhaps deserved to be. It was what she wanted, so he gave it to her. "Okay," he said. "Here it is. But it'll have to be short. I really have a lot to do."

***

After Rosenthal and Ted returned from New England, their community numbered over forty souls, ranging in age from five to sixty-eight, and the people had a wide range of expertise, from science teacher to desktop publisher to accountant to Mormon missionary to hydroponics researcher. They had, of course, hoped to find people with vital skills, but they welcomed those, like corporate lawyers and insurance agents and marketing researchers, whose skills would be completely useless, in the hope that perhaps their intelligence and experience could be dedicated to more productive ends. Rosenthal was disappointed that they had not found a suitable woman for him, but he didn't abandon hope. He knew they would go out looking for people again. There was even a man named Sal who claimed to have been a hit man for the Mafia, and whose accounts of his experiences and knowledge of weapons suggested he might be telling the truth. He said that his experiences wandering through a world filled with corpses had given him a new perspective, and he was eager to lend his skills to the enterprise of building a new society. He would later become Jamesburg's first Chief of Security, after the people of Jamesburg learned that there could still be a need for security forces for defense against human enemies in their new and sparsely populated world.

For Thomas Smith, the young man who had made his way to Jamesburg independently and said he was from Ohio, had really come from a mansion in Somerset County, New Jersey, where he, his brother, and his father had recently taken up residence. All three of them had survived the epidemic, and they, too, were starting to gather a community around themselves. Thomas' father, James Smith, had, before the epidemic, fancied himself something of a survivalist. He had even, for a brief time, tried to find and join one of the radical organizations, like Posse Comitatus, or the Order, the Sword, and the Arm of the Lord, that waged war against the government. At the time he had not pursued it very far, and he had never actually joined any of them, but he had convinced his sons to to follow him.

The living had been easy for them ever since the epidemic. They had come down out of upstate New York and had, like Rosenthal and the others, been living off of the ruins of the old world. Then, not long after taking up residence in a mansion about fifteen miles away, they discovered Jamesburg.

When Rosenthal, Ted, and the people they had found arrived back in Jamesburg, they set to work laying the foundations for their new society, and making sure they would be prepared to weather the approaching winter. Rosenthal and Mrs. Browning became the de facto leaders of the new community. They had plenty of houses to choose from, so living space was not much of a problem. They cleared out some buildings that could easily be kept cool and dry, and carefully stockpiled them with intact computers, televisions, VCRs, and other electronic equipment. "Any equipment we get may have to be kept in good repair for a long long time," Mrs. Browning pointed out. "Our descendants could be relying on these things a century from now."

After The Blue

They had also begun similarly stockpiling books, video-cassettes, and microfilms. "Any knowledge lost now may be lost forever," Mrs. Browning said. They continued stockpiling nonperishable foods, for which they had to range further than they had previously in order to accommodate the increased population. Even though they had not discovered any more rotten canned goods, it was becoming clear that they would have to begin making plans for farming and animal husbandry and food preservation within a few years. They were careful to lay in a supply of firewood for the houses that had fireplaces, along with kerosene heaters and electric space heaters they could run on batteries.

For several weeks after their return, they were all quite busy, stockpiling supplies, fixing buildings, and in general getting things in order. But they were not so busy that they failed to notice when Thomas Smith suddenly disappeared. They wondered if he had been eaten by wild dogs; if he had been ambushed by strangers hiding in the woods; if he had fallen down somewhere with a broken leg and could not get up; if he had contracted the disease months after everyone else who was susceptible had already succumbed; or even if the Gruumsbaggians had returned and were picking them off one by one. When Smith appeared two days later and said he had just 'needed some privacy' and had therefore taken a car for a little spin, they believed him, and although they weren't happy about it—they could have used his help—they just asked him to let them know the next time he planned to do something like that.

Then it happened again. This time, when he returned, they lectured him. "We're trying to build something up here," Rosenthal told him. "We're trying to preserve a modicum of civilization. But it's not going to work if we don't all cooperate. So, the choice is yours. Do you want to be a part of this community? We'd be glad to have you, if you work with the rest of us." Smith agreed and said he would refrain from unexplained absences in the future.

During his absences, Smith had been going back to the mansion where his father and brother were ensconced. They had taken in five children, all of whom they had found alone. All of them were under seven. The elder Smith liked it that way, since it made them that much easier to indoctrinate. The children were given food, and rooms to sleep in, and time to play. And their educations were not neglected. They were, each day, given teachings by the two Smiths. They were taught that they were part of the master race and that they must always obey their fuhrer, James Smith, who knew that if they would always obey him, he would have a very easy time building his own following. But, addled as he was by fascism, he still realized something essential.

"We're never going to create a master race with just the three of us and these little boys," he had told his two sons. "You boys are going to need wives." When they discovered other humans in Jamesburg, they suspected they might have found the solution to this problem. Thomas became their spy. During his absences from Jamesburg, he had, of course, returned to the mansion to report his findings.

And when Thomas made his third disappearance from Jamesburg, he took with him one of the little children who had been brought back by Rosenthal and Ted.

When the disappearances were discovered, the people of Jamesburg greeted the kidnapping, their first real crisis, with a mood of restrained panic. They gathered together near the lake in a spot on Railroad Avenue from which they had brushed some of the fallen leaves and sat outside in the brisk October sunshine. It was Mrs. Browning who spoke first. "Unfortunately, we now see we've been too trusting," she said. "It is possible that disaster and loneliness have clouded our judgment. We have to recognize that our society used to contain its fair share of psychotic individuals. We should have remembered it was inevitable some of them would be among the immune. But that must be a concern, one of our guiding principles, for the future. Our immediate concern should be how, if at all, we are to rescue little Bobby—and how we are to deal with Thomas."

"If I find him, I know how to deal with him," said Sal, and smashed his fist into his palm. "That poor little kid."

"But he could have gone anywhere," said Cynthia. "All he had to do was take a car and drive far away. We'll never find him."

Rosenthal paced among the dry leaves covering the road. Rita was so right. How could he have missed it? How could he have let himself believe everyone who had survived would be decent? And now a small child, who had been fortunate enough to survive the epidemic, to be found by adults and cared for, and to be brought to a community run by responsible people, might be endangered. If only they had any plan for finding Smith and the child, there would be some hope. He kicked angrily at the leaves. Where they had not been cleared away, the leaves covered everything in a layer of brown and orange several inches deep. Then a thought came to him.

"The leaves," he said. "They're all over the roads, and there hasn't been any wind all day. Any car would have disturbed the leaves..."

181

"Wait a minute!" Ted said excitedly. "When I was taking supplies to the warehouse on the edge of town, I thought I saw some car tracks in the leaves heading away. I didn't even think about what they were doing there!"

Rosenthal, Ted, and Sal found the tracks in the leaves, and with some difficulty, managed to trace them as far as the New Jersey Turnpike. However, the Turnpike, unlike the smaller roads, was not covered by leaves and held few clues, but they drove up and down the turnpike until they found tire tracks in piles of leaves that had accumulated on one of the off-ramps several miles north. From there, it was somewhat easier to follow the trail, although in places the road was bare and they were forced to search for several minutes until they could find it again.

The trail led them to a heavily wooded estate surrounded by a chain-link fence. They entered the property through the open gates at the entrance to a rear service road and parked the car. On foot, they made their way carefully through the woods, leaving the car concealed behind a hedgerow. After they had walked a few hundred yards, a large, white house became visible beyond the edge of the woods.

"Oh, Christ," Rosenthal said. An enormous red-and-white swastika flag hung unfurled from the roof of the house. Then he heard voices, children's voices, and he glimpsed a group of children, with swastika armbands, parading across the lawn. A middle-aged man watched them. The man was tall and trim, with a neat mustache, a thin fringe of yellow hair around the perimeter of an otherwise bald head, and wire-rim glasses. He was wearing some sort of white uniform, and he, too, had a swastika on an armband.

After The Blue

"Forward! March!" Rosenthal heard the man say to the children. They all fell into place behind him in a neat little line.

"What's going on here?" Ted whispered.

"Nasty stuff," Sal said. "We need to know how many of them there are."

"That'll have to wait," Rosenthal said. "This is a big place. There could be a lot of them in there. With all due respect, Sal, there could be too many for the three of us to handle. For now, I think we should get out of here."

The middle-aged man in the white uniform had of course been James Smith, and he had just finished giving his son Thomas a tongue-lashing for acting so quickly. There had been an inter-generational communications gap. Thomas had understood his task to be slightly different than the task James understood his instructions to have conveyed. "You idiot!" James told Thomas in his shrill voice. "You just got one! We could've gotten so many more from that place! Not only little kids, but women! And they would have done all of our work for us! Now you can't go back at all. They'll tear you apart. We've missed a marvelous opportunity!"

Later that day, Smith went outside to drill the boys. Someday, perhaps, they would be able to competently execute orders. They could at least obey orders. And one had been sharp enough to see something unusal. Rosenthal, Sal and Ted did not realize they had been glimpsed as they crouched in the woods. It was ironic, Smith thought, that the three men from Jamesburg had probably refrained from attacking his mansion for fear they would be outnumbered.

When the three men returned to Jamesburg, they convened a meeting of the entire community and told of what they had seen.

"That's it, we'll just have to pack up and go somewhere else," said Melanie Campbell, a middle-aged woman whom they had found in Toronto. "After all, they know where we are."

"We can't leave," protested Sal. "We've done too much work here already. We've got too much invested in this place."

"I think we should act first," said Ted. "We've got plenty of weapons."

"You're makin' more and more sense all the time, kid!" Sal said, punching Ted playfully on the shoulder.

"You say you don't have any idea how many of them there were?" asked Mrs. Browning.

"No. No idea," said Rosenthal.

"But all you saw was one man and several children. I think, oh, how I hate to say it, but I feel I have no choice. We have to destroy what that house represents. My older brother fought in Europe during World War II. He helped liberate some of the con-centration camps. The stories I heard...we can't let such a thing exist on the face of the Earth. We will have to kill the adults, if necessary, but I hope it will be possible to save the children. Maybe it's not too late for them. Maybe we can give them a decent home."

To hear such thoughts from Mrs. Browning, of all people, was sufficient to convince the rest of the people of Jamesburg, even those who had been in favor of leaving, of their responsibility to destroy whatever it was the mansion in Somerset County harbored. They decided they had to do it as soon as possible. So fifteen of them—all of the able-bodied men under the age of sixty—armed themselves with pistols, knives, and automatic weapons, got into cars, and headed for the mansion. They left the women, the children, and the older men in Jamesburg.

At nearly the same time, James Smith and his two sons were on their way towards Jamesburg. Now that he had been discovered, James did not feel comfortable. He had decided hastily that there was only one possible solution. He and his sons would lock the boys up in the mansion and go to Jamesburg to kill as many of the adults and older children as they could. They would drive there via a circuitous route to take the community by surprise. Smith thought it was possible that three men, armed with submachine guns, could wipe out some thirty-odd adults. The younger children could then be brought to the mansion and turned into fodder for indoctrination. And perhaps some young and pliable girls could be found and raised as brides for his sons.

In Jamesburg, Mrs. Browning stood by the window. She had realized that they were completely exposed to any attacks that might be made by the kidnappers of little Bobby, and that such attacks might very well be coming soon. It was she who organized the women and children and elderly of Jamesburg into a network of snipers and observers hidden among the buildings. And when the Smiths' car drove into Jamesburg, the place seemed to be completely desolate. The men got out of the car and carefully, their guns poised at the ready, began walking through the town.

On Railroad Avenue, near several old houses, they were confronted by an old man named Tad Dornick. Dornick, who had been found in Connecticut, was close to eighty. He had smoked all of his adult life and had terminal emphysema, and he thought that he had already contributed as much in the way of knowledge and skills to the people of Jamesburg as he could. Since he knew he did not have much longer to live anyway, he had volunteered himself as expendable, to gauge the true intentions of the invaders, although their intentions became rather obvious when he saw the weaponry they were carrying. "Hello, Thomas," he said. "May I ask why you kidnapped that boy this morning? And who are these two people with you, carrying those guns?"

Thomas started to answer, but before he could speak, his father mowed the old man down. Dornick's body, riddled with bullets, crumpled in a bloody heap on the road. That was all the signal the rest of them needed. A sudden hail of gunfire from the women and older men hidden on the second floors of the houses brought the three Smiths down. The two sons died instantly. James lingered a few hours, during which he told Mrs. Browning everything. Repentant and suddenly frightened of going to Hell, with his last breath he asked her forgiveness.

The men came back from the mansion not long afterwards. They had rescued the children, Bobby among them, and brought them back to Jamesburg. They had cut the flag with the swastika into shreds.

After that, the people of Jamesburg were cautious about the people they invited to join their community. No one they encountered in the future ever proved quite so bad, quite so thoroughly evil, though, as the Smiths. Sometimes, it almost seemed to Rosenthal that with the death of the Smiths, everything that was thoroughly evil about human beings had somehow been expunged from the planet. They found some people who had been homeless before the epidemic, but they were decent enough. And despite their newfound wariness, they kept looking for wanderers. They still needed more people.

Rosenthal and Mrs. Browning had some discussions about the next steps to take. "You know, David," Mrs. Browning said, "we really do need more people. First of all, I don't believe this group here is large enough to be genetically viable over the long term. And we still don't have a physician. I know we'll be lucky to find one at all, but we really have to try. There's still all the places to the south that we haven't checked yet."

"I know, I know," Rosenthal replied. "I'll be setting out soon. I just want to help get the others settled in here. To get things established before it gets too cold."

"I understand. But I've made a wish list of all the specialists I'd like us to have." She smiled gently as she produced a piece of looseleaf paper. "A physician, of course, and a pharmacist. More agricultural specialists, mechanics, plumbers. I know we can't afford to turn anyone away, but perhaps this list will serve to motivate you."

Rosenthal accepted the paper from her and grinned. "I know, and you want us to get some redundancy of skills. Two of the really important ones, like doctors. Just like Noah's Ark."

So, in a spirit of fun and whimsy that had long been absent from most of their hearts, the people of Jamesburg found a charter bus in good condition and spraypainted the name Noah's Ark on its side. For the next four years, except during the winter, Noah's Ark would be out on the roads, scouring the country for survivors. The people of Jamesburg would take turns, going in groups of three or four, searching the continent for living people. The first Noah's Ark

187

broke down after a while, but they replaced it easily enough with another bus. There were plenty of derelict buses. Sometimes the people they found chose not to come, but more often they did. It grew more and more difficult as time went on, as the roads deteriorated further, and more bridges and overpasses collapsed, but even as their physical world got smaller, as the wilderness reclaimed the land and closed inexorably in around them, the people of Jamesburg grew in numbers.

They would not have made it through the first winter without the nonperishable food they were able to salvage from stores. They also continued their policy of salvaging as much electronic equipment—computers, VCRs, cameras, and the like—and books and written information as they could. The things they salvaged helped bridge the period between the epidemic and the time when they became self-sufficient. And they eventually found some of the specialists they wanted.

While he felt a lingering grief for all those close to him who had died, Rosenthal plunged himself into the building of their small society with enthusiasm. It was, after all, a truly unique opportunity. They had the chance to start over, having learned from the lessons of the past, but not being ruled by the tyranny of the past. They could preserve what was valuable in the old society while jettisoning that which seemed worthless—the irrelevant institutions and stale traditions which no longer served any purpose, or which made life unnecessarily difficult or unpleasant.

Three years after the epidemic, Mrs. Browning died in her sleep. The people of Jamesburg, who now numbered five hundred and seventy-two, all mourned her passing. She had inspired them with her determination and vision. With her death, the mantle of leadership passed completely to Rosenthal, but he refused to accept any title other than Mayor. He further insisted that a council be elected on a regular basis to guide him in his decisions.

Rosenthal felt they had all been very lucky. He remembered how he had nearly given up the hope of living until he found Cynthia, and how the discovery of Mrs. Browning and her ten grandchildren, with her fierce dedication to making the best possible world for them to live in, had inspired him to build Jamesburg. And now all of these people, who had melded into a thriving community, were there because of his actions and the responses those actions had elicited from a few others. If things had happened differently, they could all still have been living solitary lives on the corpse of the old world, gradually growing more primitive, or even dying out, as the old food supplies went bad or were exhausted, and as the wilderness came back into its own.

Rosenthal had fallen in love with a woman a few years younger than himself whom they found in northern Virginia. Her name was Jennifer, and he had grown to love her more than anyone in the world. He still felt, now and then, stabs of grief for everyone he had known, for his parents and brothers and aunts and uncles and friends, but mostly he tried to let his memories of them be happy ones. And it was amazing, how so many of the people of Jamesburg seemed like his family now. He spent his days working, directing the development of all their enterprises—their farms, and their repair shops, and their procedures for preserving old machinery and information, and their systems for training the young. The evenings he spent with Jennifer, and often with friends too. Frequently they would sit around a crackling fire, talking and watching the twinkling stars, brilliant now that the city lights and the pollution were gone. Increasingly, the world of rush hours and credit card bills, of television commercials for sinus headache medication, of muggings and mortgages, seemed remote and dreamlike. He lived in a different world now. His children, when he and Jennifer had them, would never know the old world except in stories.

They stopped sending expeditions out in Noah's Ark after a few years because negotiating the roads had become increasingly difficult and besides, they were finding fewer and fewer people. Occasionally, though, strangers would, on their own, discover Jamesburg. If they chose to stay, after a careful and structured period of evaluation, they would be welcomed into the community.

The one worry they had was about the Gruumsbaggians. The people of Jamesburg generally agreed that the Gruumsbaggians must have intended to wipe out the human race, and for this they hated them. But it did not seem like the Gruumsbaggians had any more interest in the planet, or at least not in Jamesburg, and the people of Jamesburg knew that as long as the Gruumsbaggians left them alone, they would do all right.

Chapter 12

"That's an incredible story," Sheila said, when Jack had finished. "It's really fascinating." She reached out to take his hand.

He grasped Sheila's hand tentatively and then squeezed it. "It's our history," he said. "It's not a story. It's what really happened." He was glad he had taken the time to speak to Sheila. It had relaxed him after his unpleasant day spent in the office with the Gruumsbaggians. Just thinking of the traffic and the office and Captain Phillips gave him a kind of headache that he'd never had before, and Sheila was like a balm for his nerves. She was so gentle and earnest and sweet. Just to gaze into her eyes, to be with her, was enough to help him unwind. He thought how it was too bad the Gruumsbaggians insisted on a high-pressure, organized activity like the hokey-pokey for unwinding, when all that was really needed or wanted was some quiet time spent with a special person. He squeezed Sheila's hand more firmly. "But I'm glad you enjoyed hearing about it all anyway," he said, smiling.

"And now I think I have a good idea of what it is the Gruumsbaggians are trying to do, and of what happened a hundred years ago, and why they never taught us anything about Gruums-Baag. If we'd known about what happened we would have been less like the people before the epidemic, and they thought it was important to keep us the same. That's why they brought me and the others here. But—women didn't really spend the entire day baking cookies, did they?"

"Sheila, these Gruumsbaggians have gotten a lot of things very wrong. Right now I'm working on a project we hope might get them to leave. I hope it works. We can't live this way forever. I also hope that, if they do leave, they let you stay. I don't want you to go."

Sheila smiled at him, and Jack could feel the smile sweep the last lingering vestiges of tenseness away.

"I think I understand, Jack," she said. "I hope they let me stay, too." And then, even though she was sure the Gruumsbaggians would not approve, or perhaps because she was sure the Gruumsbaggians would not approve, she moved her face towards his and kissed him, tentatively at first, on the lips. He pulled her tightly to him. Then they lay down together in the sweet grass and let the fragrances of the April evening, adulterated as they were by the Gruumsbaggians' black smoke, envelop them.

***

It was hard for Jack to pull himself away from her after that, but he knew that more time spent with Sheila would mean that much less time spent on the book, and the longer the book took to be completed, the longer he and the other people of Jamesburg would be subjected to the lunatic reign of the Gruumsbaggians. He

192

had explained as much of this as possible to Sheila, and she had, at least, said she understood. Then she returned to McDonald's. She said that she still preferred to work there rather than to stay in Jamesburg and bake one sheet of cookies after another. Jack could certainly understand her feeling.

In the room above Council Hall where Jack and a few of the councilors had been preparing the book on computers and printers from before the Blue, Jack reviewed what had already been written before he got to work. Sections about the economy, disease immunity, and other facets of life in Jamesburg had already been written. Just a few sections remained to be written and then the book would be finished.

A few hours later, after he had done some editing with the help of Mayor Blanchard, Cynthia, and some of the other Councilors, a few more chapters had been set down. One chapter began:

> The Plain People of Jamesburg rarely leave their community. For example, unlike the residents of so many of the neighboring towns, they seldom work in New York City, as they are primarily employed by Jamesburg's own local enterprises. The women also work at these enterprises. Even when the women who live in the neighboring areas stay home all day baking cookies, the women of Jamesburg are out doing the same work as their men.
>
> The Plain People value a clean environment, and their lake, from which they catch many fish, is among the cleanest in the world. Similarly, their air

is generally much cleaner than the air in the rest of the state; for the Plain People have convinced the outsiders to locate their factories and highways in such a way that air pollution rarely, if ever, envelops Jamesburg. In general, the Plain People live in a way that is so different from the rest of the country that an observer from another planet might even conclude, after a cursory examination, that the Plain People are a different race entirely. With this in mind, it is odd that so little has been written about the Plain People in the past. To my knowledge, this book is the only study of its kind of the Plain People."

Jack was getting bleary-eyed, but it looked like the book might be nearly finished. It was too important an enterprise not to do right, though, so he would have to finish it the next day when he returned from work. Knowing it was nearly ready would allow him to tolerate one more day at the office.

***

The next morning Henry, Ghewen, Bob, and two other teenagers, a boy and a girl whom they had pulled out of buildings right before they destroyed them, sat in the woods feasting on muffins and rolls and orange juice and ham and milk they had taken from a supermarket after blowing out its windows with a high-powered bazooka which had knocked down a pyramid of tomato sauce cans and splattered their contents all over the floor. The supermar-

194

ket itself, however, was one of the few Gruumsbaggian-construct-
ed buildings they had seen which they had left intact. They knew
they would be returning there for supplies.

Ghewen wiped his beard with his sleeve. "We have quite a
bit more work to do this morning," he said. "Within half a mile of
here there are at least thirty-seven Gruumsbaggian buildings still
standing!" Then he laughed, a deep, rich, cheerful laugh that reverberated throughout the forest. He seemed delirious with joy.

Henry wondered, briefly, if Ghewen had cracked. Then he
decided he had never seen anyone so happy. And Henry wasn't
going to try to cure him. Henry was having too good a time himself, especially since Ghewen had made him second-in-command
of their little band. The whole thing beat staying in Jamesburg and
listening to the Gruumsbaggians, and playing the role the
Gruumsbaggians had assigned—even though he had nothing
against homosexuals, he did not share their preferences and did
not want to live that way. The girl who had joined them seemed
nice enough, and they might find others. No, he was definitely not
going to try to get Ghewen to snap out of it. Ghewen still seemed
to be in possession of his considerable intelligence; it was just that
now he was using it to blow things up.

"Do we have any specific plans for today and tomorrow?"
Henry asked. "Any special buildings you really want to get rid of?"

Ghewen held up a hand while he finished chewing a piece
of ham. "Yes," he said. "We're going to have to make a trip into
Jamesburg. I want to rescue Jenny. The thought of her there and
being made to stand on the street and solicit...I just can't let that go
on. But I'd like to do it under cover of darkness, just in case the
Gruumsbaggians are trying to get us."

"Don't you think maybe they wouldn't have much problem getting us if they wanted to?"

"Yes, I've given that some thought. Now, we know they're trying to recreate the pre-catastrophe world, correct? And we know they have some idea of what the pre-catastrophe world was like. But it's quite obvious that they have understood some of the details quite incorrectly. And remember, they're getting information, or misinformation, from our two historians, Harold and Ferdinand. I know those two very well. For all we know, they could've convinced the Gruumsbaggians that what we're doing, blowing things up right and left, was perfectly normal before the Blue."

"But what if you're wrong? What if, right now, they're sending out a team to take our guns and kill us all?" Henry was having a lot of fun, but he didn't think any amount of fun was worth death at the age of eighteen.

"That's a chance I'm willing to take. I'd rather be out here, destroying their miserable structures and maybe, just maybe, sending them a message, than over there in Jamesburg listening to them. The thought of spending the day in an office listening to a Gruumsbaggian—I'd prefer a death like this!" He stood up and slung a bandoleer over his chest. "I think I may be right about what the Gruumsbaggians are thinking, and about Harold and Ferdinand." He playfully tossed a hand grenade, the pin still in it, in Henry's direction. "Let's move out, folks!" he said. "We've got work to do!"

***

After The Blue

The next morning Jack was awakened again by the sounds of Gruumsbaggians going through the streets, yelling "Wake up! It's time for work! Wake up!" Those, however, were not the Gruumsbaggians who made him get out of bed. The Gruumsbaggian that made him get out of bed was the one that had been assigned to his father to keep him away from Jack's mother. Jack watched, through bleary eyes, as the big yellow figure herded his father into the room, and then ducked to fit under the doorframe. Jack could see two or three yellow arms snaking towards him, but before they could shake him, he sat up straight. "I'm awake, I'm awake," he said, hoping the Gruumsbaggian wouldn't touch him.

Jack and his father took their time at breakfast. Jack's mother got up to have some breakfast, too, but when she tried to sit at the same table, she was deterred by her own personal Gruumsbaggian. "You can't sit there," the Gruumsbaggian told her. "It wouldn't be right. You're divorced!"

"But what if I don't talk to him?" she said. "Would that be okay?"

When the Gruumsbaggian reminded her that any violation of divorce would most certainly be punished, she scowled and took her breakfast back upstairs to the bedroom.

After breakfast Jack and his father went to the spot by the lake where the buses had picked them up the previous day. Jack dreaded the day ahead of him, but at least the end was in sight since the book was nearly complete. They would check over it later that night and then they would give it to Roger Camiglia, who handled all of the printing in Jamesburg. Roger would put several copies on microfilm, making it look as much as possible like the film was old,

197

and they would distribute the films to conspicuous places where Gruumsbaggians might find and read them.

The trip to work was much the same as it had been the previous day. As soon as the bus passed the sign that said: "Welcome to the New Jersey Freepikeway. Speed Limit 100 Miles Per Hour," it slowed to a crawl as it entered bumper-to-bumper traffic. Again, Gruumsbaggians were all over the road, having fistfights and picnics, and generally preventing any sort of movement. It took them nearly three hours to travel the forty miles to New York City.

The only thing different about the whole morning was the demeanor of his boss, Captain Phillips. After Jack had changed into his suit, tie, and busby, Captain Phillips, wearing a suit, tie, and black sombrero, came over to his cubicle and put a protective arm around Jack's shoulder. "Tell me, Jack, is there anything bothering you?" he said, almost gently. "Is there anything I can help you with? Tell me all of your problems. I just want you to be happy. That way we all benefit."

Jack pulled himself away from the yellow arm and looked at the Gruumsbaggian curiously. "Uh, no, thank you, that's quite all right. I'm okay," he said. He wondered briefly if some new horror was behind his boss' friendliness, or if the Gruumsbaggian really felt as if bosses were supposed to act so differently from day to day. "Really, I'm fine. I'm just sitting here doing my work." Jack picked up the paper clips and began to separate them out of the little chain he had made. He knew he had another busy day of making new paper clip chains ahead of him.

***

After The Blue

"Okay, Henry," said Ghewen, "now you take Bob and Robin and go into the restaurant. Check it out. Make sure there aren't any humans inside. Then we'll blast this sucker all the way back to Gruums-Baag!"

"Right. Let's go!" Henry and the others ran, crouching, past the yellow arches and then peered through the glass doors of the McDonald's. "There's someone in there!" Henry yelled. "We're going in!"

They pulled the heavy glass doors open and slipped into the restaurant. "Sheila!" Henry said, when he saw who was behind the counter. "What are you doing here?"

"Waiting for the customers," she said. "Wow! Bob! Robin! I haven't seen you since we left Gruums-Baag! They were in my unit, Henry! Where did you..."

"No time, no time," Henry said. "We're going to blow the place up. Just a few seconds from now. Out, out, get out!"

"But what about Fred? We can't..."

"Fred? Who's Fred? Well, just make it quick."

"Okay." Sheila ran behind the counter, yelled "Fred," and a Gruumsbaggian in a blue uniform came plodding to the front of the counter.

"What is it, Sheila?" he said.

"You've got to get out! They're going to destroy the place. Hurry!"

"Oh, my. All right." The four humans and the Gruumsbaggian all exited the McDonald's.

When they got outside, Ghewen was doubly surprised. "Sheila?" he said. "You brought a Gruumsbaggian outside? What's going on?" He pointed one of the three guns he was car-

199

rying at Fred, who just looked stupefied, and began raising all four of his arms.

"No, it's all right," Sheila said. "He's with me."

"With you? *With* you?" Ghewen said, and then broke into a laugh. "Okay, but he better not try to stop us. Let's go, men!" he cried. They all backed off from the restaurant, and then they each lobbed a grenade at it. They followed with a barrage of flamethrower fire, and soon the McDonald's was a smoldering heap of twisted metal, splintered fiberglass and shattered windows.

***

Farnstarfl was beginning to wonder whether he should continue to be ecstatic or whether he should begin to be concerned about the rash of demolitions of Gruumsbaggian-built buildings happening near Jamesburg. He knew the historians said things like this had happened, but he wondered if they were aware of the scope of the violence. In an area of just twenty square miles, fifteen buildings had been demolished in the space of two days—and several Gruumsbaggians. He wondered whether he should take it as a sign of his success, or whether he should instead put a stop to it. He decided to have the human historians brought back into his office. He never actually asked them to describe to him the way things had been, because he was afraid their explanations might be unconnected to anything he or any other Gruumsbaggian had even thought of, and would make no sense to him. Instead, he asked them questions concerning particular details about the way the world was or had been. That way, he was sure to get answers he could at least partially understand.

After The Blue

"Hello, Harold. Hello, Ferdinand," he said, as the two historians were ushered into his office for the third time that day. He had become quite reliant on them, especially since they had apparently become more accustomed to talking with him. In fact, ever since realizing that Farnstarfl was not going to hurt them, they had become rather flippant with him. But neither Farnstarfl nor any other Gruumsbaggian could recognize flippancy. It was too close to sarcasm. Farnstarfl thought they were just trying to be friendly. And it never actually occurred to him to ponder whether they might be lying when they answered him. There was no such thing as lying among Gruumsbaggians. Even though he had read some human books about the phenomenon of lying, he kept forgetting whether that book had been fact or fiction.

"Don't you think it might be easier for all of us if, maybe, we just stayed here all day?" Harold said. "Then we wouldn't have to go back and forth and you wouldn't have to keep waiting for us."

"Or you could send us back to Earth," Ferdinand said hopefully.

Farnstarfl thought about Harold's suggestion for a minute. It made sense. "No, I think I prefer it like this," he said. "Anyway, I have to ask you two some questions."

"What else is new?" Harold groaned. "What is it?"

"About this violence. You're sure Earth was a violent place before the epidemic?"

The two exchanged glances. If Farnstarfl had been a better judge of human facial expressions, he might have recognized the conspiratorial winks they gave each other. But, like all Gruumsbaggians, he found it very hard to read human facial expressions; not that it was any easier for humans to do the reverse. "Like we told you, it was very violent," said Ferdinand. "There are some

201

videotapes you should see, if you can find them. I'm talking about news, of course, not fiction. Hmm...let's see. The Los Angeles riots, 1965, 1992, and 1999. Tiananmen Square in Beijing, China, in 1989. Yugoslavia, anytime between 1991 and, well, let's see..."

"Up to the epidemic," Harold said. "And then there was Hong Kong...what was the year? And Newark, 1967. Look for these films. If they're destroying things down there, then you should take it as a sign of success! It's just like it was! Now, I think we've given you plenty of help. When do you think..."

Farnstarfl cut him off with a wave of his upper left hand. "Trust me," he said. "You'll be taken back eventually. I just need your help for a while longer." He was ecstatic again. He had already seen films of one or two of the incidents they had mentioned. That being the case, the project apparently was succeeding beyond the modest aims they had expected for it by this time. He thought for a moment. They would have to fan the little surge of violence that had erupted down there in New Jersey. They would supply them with additional weapons—with tanks, and bows and arrows, and... . He tried to think of some of the other human weapons he had seen in films or read about. Aircraft carriers and atomic bombs and things. Yes. He would have to see that the humans responsible for the violence got some of those things.

"Is that it then?" said Harold. "Can we go now? Not that there's anything terribly fascinating to do in our chambers, of course." The historians had asked for translations of Gruumsbaggian books to read, but Farnstarfl refused. If humans got access to Gruumsbaggian knowledge it would be that much harder to make them live like they had before, when they hadn't known of Gruumsbaggians at all.

"No, that's not it yet," Farnstarfl said. "As you know, I've been working on the screenplay for this movie..."

"Oh yes," said Harold. "The 'Inaudible Man.' I'm sure it'll be a blockbuster hit."

"Are you still stuck at the part where the Inaudible Man goes into the restaurant and can't tell anybody what he's having?" Ferdinand asked.

"Or the part where the Inaudible Man tries to answer the phone?" Harold said.

"I have decided to abandon work on the Inaudible Man," Farnstarfl admitted. "I was not getting very far with it. But I have another idea. I have been thinking that what Jamesburg really needs is an election."

"Yes?" said Ferdinand. "So what are you going to do about it?"

"I was thinking that we might hold an election, and that I might run for Mayor against your Mayor Blanchard. What do you think?"

Harold began laughing, and by the time he stopped, tears were running down his cheeks. "Oh yes, I can see it now," he said. "In the Jamesburg Newsletter they'll have a headline that reads "Upcoming Election: Choice Between Human Being and Yellow Four-Armed Monster From Outer Space."

"Now, don't be so hasty, Harry," Ferdinand said. "They used to have headlines like that in some of the elections before the catastrophe."

"It's just a thought," said Farnstarfl. "But if I do it, I'm going to need some help from the two of you."

"Of course. Can we go now?"

Russel Like

Jack's day at work was, for the most part, quite similar to the previous one. He sat there, either staring blankly at the sides of his cubicle, or making and unmaking paper clip chains. Occasionally, Captain Phillips would come by and ask, solicitously, if there was anything he could do to help. Jack usually just asked him to go away. Around mid-morning they had another "meeting." This one lasted for almost two hours, but for Jack, it went much more quickly than the previous day's meeting, because this time he brought his paper clips.

He wondered if the ability to occupy himself with paper clips for an extended period of time was a sign that he was incredibly creative, but abandoned this line of thought when it occurred to him that it might also mean he was slowly going stark raving mad. When the meeting ended, and he returned to his cubicle, he set himself the goal of occupying his time for an hour without resorting to the paper clips. Once, he began to reach for the staples with the rationalization that playing with the staples did not count, but had enough discipline to stop himself.

A little while later Captain Phillips came over to him and put a big banana-yellow hand on Jack's shoulder. "Jack," he said, "I'm afraid we have some bad news for you."

"What is it?" Jack said, suddenly afraid. Sitting at the desk all day wearing that ridiculous outfit with that silly hat was bad enough, but at least it didn't hurt. He remembered some of the people the Gruumsbaggians had tarred and feathered.

"We're going to have to let you go."

"Let me go?"

After The Blue

"Yes. There's been a downturn in the business cycle. We just don't have the work for you anymore. But who knows? Maybe the economy will pick up. My advice to you is to hang around for a few hours. You may get lucky."

"So you're saying I should leave?" Jack could hardly believe his good fortune. Now he could return home and continue working on the book that would banish the Gruumsbaggians from Jamesburg once and for all.

"Yes. Look, Jack, I know how awful this is to hear. It's hard for me to do it. It's nothing personal. We're very happy with your work here, and hopefully we'll be able to bring you back on board soon."

Jack changed out of his suit, tie, and busby, and, paying as little attention to the elevator operator as possible, went down to street level and made his way through throngs of pushing, shoving, shouting Gruumsbaggians to the bus stop. There were no buses in sight. He waited for a while but no bus came. Then Gertrude, the Gruumsbaggian secretary in the high heels and pink dress, appeared, shouting his name. "Good news!" the alien said. "There's been an upturn in the business cycle! We have work for you again! You're to come back to the office at once!"

Jack groaned.

***

Ghewen's booming laughter reverberated off the buildings, off of the new Gruumsbaggian-built highway, and through the woods at the periphery of the parking lots as the flaming splinters of a strip mall crashed to the ground around him. He hoisted the bazooka off of his shoulder and rested it on the ground. "Direct

205

hit!" he yelled, grinning and holding his hands clasped in the air like a champion boxer.

The mall had been the standard strip mall built on the Gruumsbaggian factory planet where all strip malls were built. It had not been customized, and therefore contained the standard array of stores, including a videocassette rental store, a convenience store, a dry cleaner, and a pizzeria. It was the third strip mall Ghewen and his band had destroyed that day. In addition to the McDonald's, they had also blown up, among other things, four used-car dealerships, a gas station, and a shoe store.

The band had grown to twelve. There was Ghewen, of course, and Henry, and Sheila; and nine teenagers who had been working as clerks or janitors. Fred they had left behind near the ruins of his McDonald's. All of the humans carried weapons. "All right, everyone, let's move it out!" said Ghewen. The grin hadn't left his face, and Henry wondered again, briefly, whether the man had cracked. Then Henry reminded himself of how much fun he was having.

They got into the cars they had stolen from the Gruumsbaggians—these cars now numbered five—and drove off down the highway the Gruumsbaggians had built. Behind them stretched a line of smoldering ruins. Ahead of them lay intact buildings. But, unlike before, Ghewen drove past several of the standing structures and pulled into the parking lot of a Burger King several hundred yards further down. The other cars all followed him, and the humans piled out.

"What's that?" Henry said, pointing at the strange-looking machine standing in the parking lot. It was a drab metallic olive color, a twenty-foot long rectangle, with what looked like rubbery conveyor belts on either side. A cylindrical tube, perhaps fifteen feet in length, jutted out of the top.

"What's that?" Ghewen said. "If I didn't know better, I'd say it was an M-1 Abrams tank. And if there's no Gruumsbaggian inside, I'm going to try it out."

Ghewen soon showed them how just one little spit of gun-fire from the cylindrical tube on top could transform an intact Burger King into a pile of rubble in a matter of seconds.

***

Finally, Jack's interminable workday ended, but not before he saw Captain Phillips reading a book. On his way out, when he was fairly sure the Gruumsbaggian was not watching, Jack picked the book up and looked at it. It was called *The Nine Types of Bosses*. There were two dog-eared pages; one was to a chapter titled 'The Hard-Ass' and the other was to a chapter titled 'The Sympathizer.' Jack looked at the table of contents. There were numbers next to each chapter. There was a one next to the 'Hard-Ass,' and a two next to the 'Sympathizer.' Suddenly Jack realized why his boss had been so harsh the previous day and so accommodating the next. Jack wondered if bosses before the Blue had really been so changeable. There was a three next to the 'Jerk,' and a four next to the 'Mentor.' And next to the chapter entitled the 'Paranoid Megalomaniac' was a five. Jack made a mental note to bend heaven and earth not to come in on day five.

There were two tarred and feathered figures on the bus on the way home. This time Jack and his father were on the same bus, as was Jack's older brother. Again, they each had a copy of a newspaper at their seats. The headline read "Evidence Now Suggests That JFK was Shot by Elvis." Another front-page article was entitled "Elvis and JFK Sighted Together in Paris with the Queen of England." After the three-hour trip home through the traffic and the half hour he had to spend doing the hokey-pokey in the thick black smoke near the lake, Jack was ready to collapse, but he forced himself to go to the workroom above Council Hall. He and the councilors he was working with reviewed what they had put together, and brought it down to the Hall for the entire council to review.

"You all know what we are doing here," Mayor Blanchard said. For some reason he was still wearing a busby. Jack wondered if he had just forgotten to take it off after leaving the office, or if he actually liked wearing it. "We have, we believe and hope, completed a project that will force the Gruumsbaggians to leave us alone in Jamesburg. After you have all had a chance to review the material, we will bring it over to the printing facility. Roger has been alerted and he is prepared to make up microfilms of it this very night. Then we will have to distribute them. Are there any questions?"

"I have a question," said Barbara Noler with a sneer. "Where is Desmond? This was his bright idea."

"You know what they tried to do to him, Barbara," Martin Oversee said. "Would you have stayed?"

"Oh, yes, I see. He foists this cockamamie scheme upon us and then leaves all the work for us to do. How nice of him."

"Well, Barbara," said Cynthia, "if you have a better idea, please share it with us. I'd love to hear it. Or would you like to spend every day for the next forty years baking fourteen trays of cookies?"

Barbara Noler did not answer. She had other plans.

After The Blue

There have always been people like Barbara Noler, who are petty and jealous and spiteful, people who will do anything in their power to prevent others from succeeding. Most of these people grow up, after a while, and learn to accept and even appreciate the good fortune of others, but Barbara Noler was not one of these. Perhaps in a larger community her intense emotions could have been sublimated to other ends, such as career goals, or possibly some hobby. Or maybe she would have been a hermit. Maybe her strange emotional state was the product of inbreeding. Whatever the cause, her actions were to have immediate repercussions for the people of Jamesburg.

For after Jack and the Mayor and the Councilors had reviewed the book, sent it to the printer, and made plans to put copies of the microfilm in conspicuous spots, Barbara made a visit to the Gruumsbaggians and told them everything. She told them about the book that had been written and how it was meant to deceive the Gruumsbaggians. She told them this deception was bothering her conscience, and that she could not live with the ruse.

***

Farnstarfl was fascinated when he received a microfilm of the book about the Plain People of Jamesburg. He found it incredible that such a group of people could survive amid the civilization that the humans had created in New Jersey and New York. But if this were accurate, it meant he would have to proceed differently with the Earth Project in regard to the community in Jamesburg. This was certainly something that called for help from the two human historians.

209

After he had allowed Harold and Ferdinand to read over the material, he asked them whether it was accurate or not. They looked knowingly at one another. "Um, oh yes, very accurate," Harold said, with a straight face.

"We've been trying to tell you about this all along," said Ferdinand, "but you wouldn't let us."

Farnstarfl sent them back to their chambers and paced back and forth in his office, wringing his lower left with his upper right hand. Was it possible that he had made a mistake, and in his fervor to reconstruct pre-epidemic Earth had irrevocably damaged the last vestige of true Earth civilization?

Then Barbara Noler was brought in, still a bit shaken from the shuttle trip from Earth to the orbiting Command Center, but eager to speak. "Most High, this human says that book you've just read was a device intended to deceive us and send the Earth Project in the wrong direction," said one of her Gruumsbaggian escorts.

"What? What is this? Tell me. I must know," Farnstarfl said. He stopped wringing his hands and stood staring at Barbara.

***

The next day the people of Jamesburg woke up to find that a new sign had been placed everywhere. It read 'The Writing of New Books is Forbidden Until Reality Has Been Established. By Orders of the Governor. Violators Will Be Punished.'

Chapter 13

Farnstarfl still found it hard to accept that the humans had tried to deceive him. Why, when his goals were their goals? He was only trying to rebuild what the humans, when given the chance, had built for themselves. And those two human historians! They had lied to him, too! They said the book was completely true. But the female had come and was able to prove beyond a shadow of a doubt that the book was a total fabrication. It was a major setback to the Earth Project.

The evidence that the historians had lied did not, however, make Farnstarfl discount the other things they had told him. Lying, like fiction, was so alien to the Gruumsbaggian psyche that it did not occur to Farnstarfl to think that perhaps, since the historians had lied to him this once, they might have lied about other things as well. So the flow of tanks and other weapons to Ghewen and his band was not interrupted.

Farnstarfl was not so much miffed at learning that the humans had tried to deceive him as he was puzzled. After all, the ultimate goal of the Earth Project was to restore the intricacy and beauty of the old Earth civilization. Farnstarfl knew that the present-day humans would learn to like it again—how could they not, when the Gruumsbaggians were just restoring what the humans' ancestors had chosen to build? But only now was he guessing that the achievement of his goal might take a while. In his research he had come across the term 'acquired taste' more than once. He wondered if pre-epidemic Earth were an acquired taste.

**

Back on Earth, Jack was sitting in a stationary bus on the New Jersey Freepikeway in the middle of a cloud of black smoke. The bus was not moving because it was blocked by the cars all around it. The huge cloud of black smoke had engulfed the bus several minutes earlier and now completely obscured the sun. "Those two Gruumsbaggians at the house won't even let me talk to your mother, much less touch her," complained his father, who was sitting next to him. "They still insist we're divorced."

Jack had ceased to care. He was in a bleak, desolate mood of his own. Earlier in the morning, as he got ready for 'work,' he had been happy, almost lighthearted, anticipating the departure of the Gruumsbaggians as soon as they found the book. Then he saw the signs about the writing of new books and the establishment of reality and he knew, with a terrible sinking feeling, that their effort to deceive the Gruumsbaggians into leaving Jamesburg had, for whatever reason, failed. That was it, then. He could look forward to a miserable farce of a life, spending four or five hours fighting traffic every day, sitting in an office doing nothing except taking abuse from a yellow, four-armed monster from outer space, and then having to do the hokey-pokey when he came home.

There was one bright spot, though. Perhaps he would be able to marry Sheila. Perhaps there would be one glimmer of true happiness in his life. But then he decided the Gruumsbaggians would probably come up with some ludicrous reason why he couldn't marry her. "She's not your type," he could imagine them saying, or "the two of you have different signs."

The bus lurched forward several feet. "Oh, there we go," his father said. "I hope we get there soon. We've got such important work to do."

"Oh yeah. I've made every possible type of paper-clip chain you could ever imagine." Suddenly Jack remembered Henry. He hadn't seen him for several days. Jack had been so caught up in the book that he had not even thought of his friend. What was it Henry had said—that he was going to join Ghewen? He hadn't seen Ghewen in several days, either. He wondered what they were up to. He hoped and prayed it might be something that could help them all, even if he wasn't quite sure what they could do. It was his only hope.

***

Farnstarfl had called the two historians into his office. "So I now understand you two lied to me about that book," he said.

Harold's face assumed an expression of exaggerated false contrition. "Oh, we did? I'm so sorry," he said. "It must have been some sort of mistake."

"I'm afraid I'm going to have to send you back to Earth," Farnstarfl said.

"What?" Ferdinand said. "You mean that's it? All we had to do was lie to you and you'd send us back?"

"Now I know that I can't..." Farnstarfl fumbled for the word. It represented another concept that was completely alien to Gruumsbaggians, because it had to do with truth, and lying, and fiction. He let his sentence dangle in silence for several seconds while he tried to recall the word. "Trust!" he said finally. "I just can't trust you anymore. Therefore I have no choice but to send you back to Earth."

"Well, that's, that's awful!" Harold said, and again, his sarcasm was lost on Farnstarfl.

"On Earth, of course, you will both be expected to live like the other humans," Farnstarfl said.

"That hardly sounds like a punishment to me," said Ferdinand. Of course, he had not been to Earth in a while, since before much of the Earth Project had been implemented.

After he saw the two historians off, Farnstarfl began to wonder about the human who had alerted them to the danger of the false reality that the Gruumsbaggians had almost put into effect. She should, he decided, get some sort of special status among the humans, and he knew just what status that was. For he had begun to learn about something the humans had in the past called 'celebrities.' It seemed to him like everyone wanted to be a celebrity—that celebrities were truly the luckiest of all the humans, and that the idolization of celebrities had been an important part of pre-epidemic Earth.

He had contemplated sending Gruumsbaggians into Jamesburg dressed as movie stars, but then he had a hard time figuring out how the humans could be forced to demand a Gruumsbaggian's signature. Most Gruumsbaggians couldn't even hold a pen or pencil because their hands weren't designed properly. In his research into celebrities, he had watched a videotape of a woman who seemed to be a celebrity. She was up on a stage and was surrounded by cheering fans. She had short, platinum-blonde hair, and she wore very little—just little white panties and things on her breasts shaped like lollipops—and as she leaned over to face the crowd and gyrated her hips, she sang something about being like a virgin. That was how the song had begun. After the song was finished, a voice announced "There she is, and girls, we know you want to grow up to be just like her..."

The more he thought about it, the more he liked the idea. It was time to start bringing celebrities back to Earth. And who better to bestow the status upon than the one who had helped them prevent a false reality? Farnstarfl felt his three hearts bubble in expectation. Things were working out after all.

***

If Farnstarfl had known how many other false realities were incubating in Jamesburg, he might even have been tempted to wipe the whole place off of the map. For the signs about the writing of books and the establishment of reality, and general gossip about the council's plan, had made the council's plan clear to everyone in Jamesburg. And very few of the people of Jamesburg were satisfied with the state of affairs. They began to gather ideas for their own books, for false realities of their own they hoped the Gruumsbaggians could be convinced to make real. Some of the false realities were not terribly altruistic.

For example, one older man, who had never been quite content with his lot in Jamesburg, began to think of grander things. He had recently read a book about the pre-catastrophe British royal family. He had been quite taken with the way the royal family lived—servants, castles, public adoration, virtually unlimited quantities of money, sumptuous meals—and the whole incident with the Gruumsbaggians and the establishment of new realities gave him an idea.

He would write a book in which he would demonstrate that he, himself, was the sole living descendant of the royal family. Upon reading it, he felt sure, the Gruumsbaggians would take him to a castle and lavish him with food and women and liquor and money.

He made one mistake, though. He began writing his book on a pad of paper on a park bench—outside—under a street light, after he finished doing the hokey-pokey. Several Gruumsbaggians saw him sitting there, writing things down.

They had their orders, and they immediately confiscated the paper. Then they told him, in no uncertain terms, how the writing of new books posed a grave threat to the establishment of reality, and that he would have to be punished for what he had done.

After he finished getting all of the tar and feathers off of himself, he decided it just wasn't worth it. He would live out the rest of his life like the rest of the people of Jamesburg.

But he was just one person, and a foolish and reckless one at that for having written outside. There were many others who were writing whenever Gruumsbaggians were not around. All over Jamesburg imaginations were at work, some of them in the service of the community, some of them purely in the service of self, but all of them had at least one goal in common—the deception of the Gruumsbaggians.

**

Jack went through the day as if in a daze. He had been so certain the book would deceive the Gruumsbaggians, yet there he was again, sitting in an office, wearing a busby, and playing with paper clips. His Gruumsbaggian boss was acting, as the chapter in the book said, like a 'Jerk.' Jack knew he would be able to tolerate the next day, when his boss planned to act as a 'Mentor,' but he was increasingly worried about the day after that, when his boss planned to be a 'Paranoid Megalomaniac.'

That evening, when he got off the bus and the Gruumsbaggians led him along with the other passengers to the hokey-pokey site near the lake, he was too depressed even to really think about what he was doing. When he saw Barbara Noler up on a podium, though, he was startled. She was scantily dressed and her flaccid body flushed pink. She looked alternately embarrassed, sullen, and enraged, but the two Gruumsbaggians flanking her prevented every attempt she made to leave the stage. "Now sing or you'll be punished," Jack heard one of them say to her.

The two Gruumsbaggian guards, like most of the menial Gruumsbaggians who had been sent to work on the Earth Project, were not really all that smart. They did not understand that Barbara was supposed to be standing up on the podium as a reward. They only understood that she was supposed to be up on the podium, singing, and wearing next to nothing.

Faintly, she began. "Like a virgin..." she shouted, in a creaky, hesitant voice, and did not continue until further prodding by one of the guards. All of the men who had just gotten off of the bus stopped to gape at her until one of the blue-uniformed Gruumsbaggians shouted, "All right, time to start unwinding. Get in a circle, everyone, and....You put your left foot in! You take your left foot out!"

They had been listlessly moving to the music of the hokey-pokey for several minutes, their voices barely audible because Barbara Noler's scratchy, unwilling voice was being broadcast at tremendous volume for the entire town to hear, when Jack first saw the tank. Suddenly, the sound of Barbara Noler's voice disappeared. For a brief moment, the sounds of "you put your right hand in and you shake it all about" could be heard and then they too faded away. Only the sounds of distant gunfire crackled in the night air. Soon, though, that sound was eclipsed by a babble of voices, and the hokey-pokey site near the lake was abruptly a confused mess of men and Gruumsbaggians running this way and that to avoid the tank, which was spitting some sort of glowing projectile every few seconds. Screams and cries and more confusion could be heard in the distance.

Jack looked back and forth wildly, fascinated by the tank. He had read a little bit about them in some of his history training sessions, but when the tank headed straight for him, he stood there, as if transfixed by the cylindrical tube. Briefly, in a flash of lucidity, he wondered if this was the way the Gruumsbaggians had decided to kill him for his part in writing the book.

After The Blue

The tank stopped a few feet in front of him. He was so shocked when Henry and Sheila and three other humans emerged from it that for a moment he was sure he was dreaming. "Jack!" Henry said. "Get in! Come with us! But hurry up. We have to meet Ghewen and the others in just four minutes. They went to get Jennifer. His wife, you know. Come on! We've been having so much fun!"

"Wha...What's going on?" Jack answered him. "I'm sorry. I'm very confused."

"Just get in, Jack," Henry insisted. "We'll fill you in."

Once he was inside the tank, and after they had told him a little bit about what was going on, Jack had an idea. "We have to get the printer. You know, Roger Camiglia? And all of his equipment, or at least the stuff for making microfilms. There still might be some hope." It was a long shot, but he could see no alternative. They would have to try again. Maybe the next book would be a success.

It did not take them long to find Roger, who was at the printing office a few blocks away. And so, in addition to Jack, and Ghewen's wife Jennifer, and several dozen other Jamesburg citizens, Roger Camiglia and his printing equipment ended up joining Ghewen's growing band in the woods. The tank rumbled away from Jamesburg, leaving behind it a demolished podium, an obliterated pollution-generating machine, and several dead Gruumsbaggian guards.

There was rubble all over the hokey-pokey site near the lake, but otherwise, within a few minutes of the departure of the tank, a calm settled over the darkness of the April evening. A few crickets even chirped tentatively.

219

Then, from all directions, Gruumsbaggians slowly began to converge on the site. They had known that at some point, religion would have to be brought back to Earth, religion like it had been in the past. They had waited for a while, in part because they had a hard time understanding what religion was all about. But they sensed that now, after the scene of violence and devastation that had taken place, was an appropriate time to introduce more spiritual concerns. After all, it seemed like a somber, spiritually meaningful moment.

And so they strode into the area near the lake. There were a number wearing big red coats, curly white wigs, and great big shaggy white beards. "Ho ho ho," they said repeatedly, as they picked their way over the fragments of the podium. Several others, who wore white bunny suits, had confused the White Rabbit with the Easter Bunny. "I'm late! I'm late for a very important date!" they would say to any humans they passed on the way, and then follow this with "Here, have an egg." There was another Gruumsbaggian who had donned an outfit that made him look like a tooth with wings. Others wore green leotards and tried to speak with brogues, while others dressed as pumpkins, and still others appeared in the guise of large red hearts with arrows through them. There was even one in a groundhog costume.

As they all trod slowly over the wreckage, under the clear, moonlit coolness of the April night, the big four-armed figures in their various costumes began to sing. At first they sang in a low, murmuring sound, but then they let their voices gradually rise to full strength. They sang with as much feeling and reverence and devotion as Gruumsbaggians possibly could. "Silent night," they began. "Holy night...."

Chapter 14

When he learned that there were other humans attempting to introduce additional false realities into the Earth Project through the writing of books, Farnstarfl at first considered not getting any more information from books at all. They had already made quite a bit of progress in the Earth Project, anyway. After all, they had reconstituted the economy of Old Earth, and the rudiments of the lifestyle, and some of what had apparently been called 'social ills,' and the resource constraints and environmental pollution that had been so influential. To avoid incorporating any false realities into the Project, they could just leave things as they were.

But he found himself forced to reject this strategy. A major reason for the Earth Project was the marvelous complexity, the beautiful intricacy of every facet of the civilization of Old Earth, and to stop now, with just what they had already done, would be to only go half-way. He thought back to his Gruumlethood, and remembered how, with one of the flaxzen-mours he had taken apart, he had lost half of the pieces before he had been able to reassemble it. He had reassembled what he could, but the finished product was somehow unsatisfying. He had thrown it out.

His decision to proceed having been made, Farnstarfl contemplated which aspects of life on Old Earth should come next. It seemed like there were a million little things. Smoking, for example. He didn't quite understand the appeal, but it would be necessary to start making the humans of Jamesburg smoke cigarettes and, of course, the Gruumsbaggians who were in the 'parents' role would have to start smoking so the human children who were their charges would grow up in a more authentic atmosphere. His researchers informed him that the people of Jamesburg had no tobacco cigarettes, although apparently a few of them smoked another plant, which they called marijuana and grew themselves, on rare occasions. So one thing the Gruumsbaggians had to do was start manufacturing cigarettes. Then he remembered they had already placed advertisements for cigarettes on a number of billboards and animals, and he was happy. That would make it easier to introduce cigarettes, he felt sure.

And there were other aspects of society they had yet to re-introduce, too. Humans had apparently had organizations, things called 'clubs,' for all sorts of special interests. They would have to start organizing the humans into clubs.

Also, there were other forms of entertainment besides television shows and the hokey-pokey, Farnstarfl remembered. For example, there had been people called 'stand-up comedians' whose job, as far as Farnstarfl could tell, was to get up in front of large crowds and talk angrily about other people who went to express supermarket checkout lines with more than twelve items. This whole system made very little sense to Farnstarfl, especially as his researchers had been unable to even determine what precisely express supermarket checkout lanes were, but stand-up comedians were a part of the past so they would have to be a part of the future.

And of course there were other forms of amusement—like board games. Farnstarfl had already played the one called *Monopoly* with Harold and Ferdinand. He kept ending up in jail. There had been other facilities for recreation—things like amusement parks—which the Gruumsbaggians had finally figured out were not for transportation only after they had built a commuter log flume from Philadelphia to Washington. And there were gambling casinos, another activity which Farnstarfl still didn't understand.

There were so many idiosyncratic things the humans had done—so many details. And the Gruumsbaggians would have to recreate every one of them. When the Gruumsbaggians completed the Earth Project and left Earth to the humans, at some time in the distant future, the Gruumsbaggians would have guided the humans into a state almost exactly like the one they had lived in before the epidemic. He was still pretty sure of that.

***

The little spot of woods that had not been cut down by the Gruumsbaggians had become the base of operations for Ghewen and his band. But what with all the tanks that they had found, and all of the new people they had taken from Jamesburg in the raid, along with the teenagers they kept finding in the stores they blew up, the little woodland was getting quite crowded.

The raid had been extremely successful. It had accomplished its primary objective, the rescue of Ghewen's wife. They found her on a street corner, wearing a very short skirt, with a Gruumsbaggian guard continually prompting her to say, "Hey babe, wanna have some fun?" to every passing male. The raid had also succeeded in demolishing the pollution machine. There were still clouds of black smoke wafting around, of course, because the Gruumsbaggians had constructed many pollution machines, but in the immediate vicinity of Jamesburg the air was no longer the same choking black miasma that it had been.

The morning after the raid, Henry explained to Jack the whole sequence of events that had led to the formation of the band and the raid on Jamesburg. Jack, in turn, told Henry about how it was to work in a Gruumsbaggian office and how the book had failed to deceive the Gruumsbaggians. Sheila was there, listening, and marveling at how her life had changed. It seemed to her that life had become one long cascade of different realities slipping into one another, from the original version she had been taught on Gruums-Baag, to the one she discovered on Earth, to the version Jack told her, and now to her life as a member of an outlaw band hiding in the woods. She was certain of only two things: that the Gruumsbaggians were not to be trusted and that there was a bond between herself and Jack. The story he had told her, of Jamesburg's founding after the Blue, had captivated her as no Gruumsbaggian story or lesson ever had. Jack's story was sincere and profound, and she felt she could trust him. But when she looked at him, she knew her feelings for him transcended mere gratitude.

"All I know, Henry," he was saying, "from what you've said, if I stay with you here I won't have to go back to that horrible office. Did I mention that my 'boss' is planning to act like a para-noid megalomaniac the day after tomorrow?"

"Yeah? Well, you better stick with us," Henry said. "Like I said, I'm not sure if Ghewen's cracked or what, but it's been a whole lot of fun. You should see these little malls after you lob a hand grenade at them and then the little pieces of wood fall all around you. It's so "cool," to use one of your historical words."

"The only thing I wonder, though," Jack said, "is how long the Gruumsbaggians are going to let this continue. You say that they don't seem to mind?"

"Mind? They've been giving us these tanks! They want us to do this! Ghewen thinks it has something to do with them wanting to recreate the violence on Earth before the Blue."

"But assuming they do let us keep doing this, we can't do it forever. What kind of life would that be?"

Henry was nonplused for a moment. "I guess you're right. It will get old after a while, won't it? But what's the alternative? I can see how happy you were living the way they wanted you to live, sitting in their traffic and then sitting in that office all day. I'd rather be doing this. I think you would, too."

"You're right about that. But think about it this way. If they want us to do this stuff, just like they want us to sit around in traffic and in offices, we're still being manipulated by them, or by what they perceive the past to have been like. But just because I like to study the past doesn't mean I want to live in it. I don't want my life to be ruled by the past. I want to live my life the way I choose to. And I think there's still a chance. That's why I insisted that we get Roger and the printing equipment."

"Oh, I see," Henry nodded. "You're going to write another book. Why do you think they'll fall for this one if they didn't fall for the last one?"

"Well, they might not fall for it," Jack admitted. "But I don't know exactly what tipped them off last time. Who knows? Maybe someone gave it away. Anyway, I have to try. Otherwise, they'll control us forever. And who knows what they have planned for us? Maybe they think anyone who's been involved in a war should be executed eventually."

Henry was visibly shaken. "Good point. So what is the book going to be about, this time?"

"Excuse me, boys," Barbara Noler said with a wry smile as she positioned herself next to them. She had been taken out of Jamesburg when the podium was destroyed, and she had been given a new set of clothes. "I couldn't help overhearing part of your conversation."

"And?" Jack said.

The smile disappeared from her face. "You were right, before," she said. "About how they found out about the book."

"I was?"

"When you said that someone might have told them. That someone was...I'm afraid it was me. I want to apologize. It was a stupid, childish, and destructive thing. The Gruumsbaggians wouldn't have known the book was false and I don't think there's any reason why they couldn't be fooled again." She dropped her eyes. "I know you must hate me. I can't imagine...but I'm not the same person who went to the Gruumsbaggians...I didn't know...I feel like I owe a debt to Desmond for rescuing me. I want to help all of you. What can I do? Please."

Jack's mind was spinning with surprise and anger, but he could see that taking revenge on Barbara would not make the Gruumsbaggians go away. And if what she said was true—and he had no reason to doubt her—maybe another book really might have a chance at working. He was about to speak when Ghewen's voice rang out among the trees. "Gather round, everyone! Time for a strategy session. Time to plan the next raid!"

"This changes things," Jack said, as they walked over to heed Ghewen's call.

***

That evening the Gruumsbaggians held the first meetings of special interest clubs in Jamesburg. The Gruumsbaggians recruited members at random from the streets, and even from inside people's houses, under threat of punishment. In one of the groups, which actually met inside Council Hall on Railroad Avenue, about twenty humans sat around the table and listened to a Gruumsbaggian in a purple frock coat lecture them about the spiritual value of backyard carrot farming. In another building on Railroad Avenue a Gruumsbaggian wearing a conical black hat and studded diamond rings on every finger of all four hands tried to explain the details of how to make a fortune through door-to-door ice cream sales to a captive audience of thirty or forty middle-aged men. In still another building, a Gruumsbaggian with towels dangling from his shoulders and a pair of sunglasses pushed up against his bright yellow forehead was explaining to his humans the proper way to sit on the beach and enjoy the sunshine. And in one of the meeting rooms in Jamesburg, a Gruumsbaggian lecturer, wearing a T-shirt emblazoned with a picture of a flying saucer with a diagonal line drawn through it, was telling a group of humans who had been appointed the 'UFO skeptics club' why the evidence for the existence of UFOs was fallacious; why there could not possibly be such a thing as UFOs or life in outer space; and why anyone who said otherwise was either sadly misinformed or insane.

227

"Now we at the UFO Skeptics Club," the Gruumsbaggian said, "do not believe any of these accounts of little green men from other planets coming to Earth. What evidence do we have that UFOs are real? None! I for one simply don't believe life can exist on other planets, and I'm sure you will all agree with me."

"Wait a minute," one of the men in the meeting room said. "How can we not believe in creatures from outer space when you're standing right here in front of us?"

"What are you trying to say?" the Gruumsbaggian said.

"Well, you're an alien..."

"Are you telling me that I'm not a human being?"

"You do have four arms and a big red nose..."

"Oho! Now we have no tolerance for diversity! And I'm just as human as you are. Anyway, we should get back to our topic. And I don't want to hear any more about this 'alien' bit, or you may have to be punished."

The man frowned and threw up his hands. "Fine," he said. "You're as human as I am. Please go on."

***

Because Ghewen's band of marauders had grown rather numerous since its visit to Jamesburg, the next raid was quite spec-tacular. They had found a stretch of highway to the north which the Gruumsbaggians had lined with fast-food restaurants, strip malls, dance clubs, shoe stores, insurance offices, and warehouses. Ghewen and his band now had a half dozen tanks, scores of cars, and enough rifles, semi-automatics, hand grenades, pistols, bazookas, and flamethrowers to equip everyone. After a sumptuous dinner of luncheon meats, colas, cakes, pies, and Twinkies they had stolen from the nearby Gruumsbaggian-built supermarket they were using for supplies, they headed north.

It was Jack's first raid. After they had blown up about twelve or thirteen buildings, and after the nagging fear he had that the Gruumsbaggians were going to come and haul them all away had ebbed, he began to appreciate the spectacle they had created. For several miles behind them, the highway was lined on either side by blazing fires. The stores had been empty, and the scene was almost beautiful. But Jack could not help wondering how long the Gruumsbaggians would allow this to continue. He could not see how they would go to all the effort to construct these things and then let them be destroyed so quickly, although it was obvious that they did not always make sense in what they did. He felt, ultimately, that there was only one way out of the entire situation the Gruumsbaggians had forced upon them—to feed them misinformation. He began making mental notes for the next book he was going to write. He had to try. He had to do his best to free Earth from the Gruumsbaggians.

This time he was going to try to convince the Gruumsbaggians that their entire effort was futile and pointless. He was going to try to make the Gruumsbaggians think that what they were doing was, in effect, redundant, that there was no reason to restore what had existed before the Blue because much of it, too, was an artificial construct; and therefore the entire enterprise was pointless.

He found it much easier to prepare himself mentally for this book than for the first one. The work he had done on the first book had liberated his imagination. He was no longer content to live in a reality of someone else's making. He was going to make his own.

Russel Like

Jack was not entirely aware of it, since he had spent virtually no time in Jamesburg since the failure of the first book, but he was in competition with numerous other potential realities. But the Gruumsbaggians were weeding out the competition as best they could through their prohibition on writing in Jamesburg.

One of the potential realities came from a man in Jamesburg named Fischer. Several years earlier, he had discovered the old religious works of the twentieth-century evangelists and had been "saved." He had proselytized and proselytized to the people of Jamesburg, but few listened. They generally already had their own religious beliefs, if they wanted any at all, and they were not receptive to his preachings. But now he saw his opportunity. He began writing a book that described the fervently religious nature of the human race before the Blue, about how everyone felt so incredibly strongly about their faith and about their savior that they subordinated all other aspects of life to Him.

Fischer did not have the good luck to finish his book. One morning, when the Gruumsbaggians were coming by his house to make him go to his office in New York City, they discovered him to be already awake, busily scribbling away. They confiscated and destroyed his manuscript and reminded him that the writing of new books was prohibited until reality was established. Then they punished him. After the feathers had fallen out and the tar-like substance dried, and the chips had flaked off of his skin, he began again.

After The Blue

The next time they discovered him writing, not only did they punish him, but they also assigned him a round-the-clock Gruumsbaggian guard. As soon as he picked up a piece of paper it would be plucked from his hand and shredded. The vigilance of the Gruumsbaggians in the defense of what they were sure was reality knew no bounds.

***

Farnstarfl's decision to go ahead, full steam, with the reconstitution of all facets of Earth life meant that higher education could not be neglected. All over the world, in places where there was evidence that they had existed before, the Gruumsbaggians began establishing universities. They had done this in New Brunswick, New Jersey, with the university closest to Jamesburg—Rutgers. The Gruumsbaggians knew they would have to start sending young men and women to these universities, and they knew the children who were being brought up by Gruumsbaggians would also, eventually, need to go to college.

Some Gruumsbaggians had taken the role of professors, of course. And they were not neglecting their research. At Rutgers, one of the professors was exploring the role of meteorites in world history. Another was researching the intricate and delicate relationships between the practice of astrology and the celebration of Groundhog Day. Still others were investigating the reasons for the decline of the rutabaga as a food source and the concomitant rise of the turnip. The impact of shoelace manufacturing on world trade deficits and the role of people named 'Bob' in American politics were also being researched by Gruumsbaggian specialists. In general, the Gruumsbaggians were establishing research departments in virtually every field of academic endeavor.

231

When their students were ready, the Gruumsbaggian professors would have much to teach them.

**

When Farnstarfl learned of the destruction of every building on a ten-mile stretch of the highway they had built, he began to wonder whether or not he was allowing the fugitives and outlaws to go too far. He wished, for a moment, that he still had his trusty human historians to refer any questions to, but then remembered that he had expelled them. It was so hard for him to figure out just how much violence was enough! He went back and watched the videotaped accounts of the several Los Angeles riots, the disintegration of the country the humans called Yugoslavia, the suppression of Hong Kong, and of other violent events. He soon realized it was very hard to determine from these images just how much violence there had actually been.

While there had hardly been anyone, it seemed, trying to stop the violence in Los Angeles, in many places one group of humans tried to keep another group from damaging things and being violent. His mind was made up.

If there were any more major outbreaks of violence he would have to send a battalion of Gruumsbaggians, armed like human police, to put a stop to it.

**

The next morning, after a raid on the local supermarket to get breakfast, Ghewen assembled his band, which now numbered nearly one hundred, and gave them a rousing speech full of congratulations and exhortations. "Last night was wonderful, truly wonderful!" he boomed, and the crowd cheered. His wife Jennifer stood up and gave him a passionate hug. When she was done, he held up his hands to signal the crowd to quiet down, which they did. "Now, I think we're ready to tackle the biggest target yet! We're going to attack one of the biggest structures the Gruumsbaggians have for miles and miles around. We are going to transform it into a shapeless pile of bricks and mortar! Because of its size, it will take some planning, but I think we're up to it.

"Jack and Henry, you should both know what I'm talking about. The place where we first learned that that vile extraterrestrial race had returned to Earth.

"What I'm saying is this: in two days, we are going to knock the Mall of Freehold into the ground!"

The crowd went wild.

Chapter 15

The next day was bright and sunny. Only a few puffs of black smoke from one of the Gruumsbaggian pollution machines marred the beauty of the April morning, and Jack was hard at work. He had begun writing the next book with Ghewen's support and approval. "So how's it coming?" Ghewen asked when he took a break from his preparations for the upcoming raid. "Is this going to be the one to finally evict the Gruumsbaggians from our planet once and for all?"

"I certainly hope so," said Jack, looking up from the pad on which he was scribbling his notes. "If this doesn't work...Are you sure you don't want to help me with this one?"

Ghewen shook his head slowly. "I'm sorry, Jack. I just couldn't concentrate on something like that now. Just two weeks ago it wouldn't have been a problem, but now my ire's up. There's no way I could ever concentrate. You should know, though, you have my complete support. I want this to succeed as much as you do—maybe more."

Jack's spirits were buoyed by Ghewen's support. He saw this, now, as the only way they would ever escape from the con-

234

trol of the Gruumsbaggians. Even in their destruction of the buildings, Jack knew they had been manipulated—after all, the
Gruumsbaggians had provided them with tanks!—and he did not
like it. The only way out of it was to manipulate them back. He
hoped the book he was writing would do that. In the book, he
wrote about a third race, not human and not Gruumsbaggian,
which had had an effect on Earth. If this didn't work, he didn't
know what he would do. The remnants of the human race would
be doomed to live under any reality the Gruumsbaggians determined to fashion for them.

***

In Jamesburg itself, the Gruumsbaggians were having a
fairly easy time controlling realities. Their presence in the town
was simply too pervasive. If false realities were not discovered
by the Gruumsbaggian squads which awakened everyone in the
morning, then they were discovered by the Gruumsbaggians who
monitored the women baking cookies in the houses, or by the
Gruumsbaggians who had been assigned to particular humans to see
that they behaved like divorcees, or homosexuals, or hypochondri-
acs, or petty criminals, or whatever the Gruumsbaggians had determined they should act like. The Gruumsbaggians had nipped in the
bud realities in which the Gruumsbaggians engaged in a civil war
and slaughtered one another; several in which the writer of the reality was showered with riches and power and adulation; one in which
the people of Jamesburg were each given several Gruumsbaggians
to act as personal slaves; and one in which the Gruumsbaggians
decided to interact only with humans in what had been Bulgaria,
among others.

The first offenders were, of course, tarred and feathered. Subsequent violations of new realities were met with the attachment of a Gruumsbaggian guard to the individual. There were now several people in Jamesburg who were stalked, wherever they went and whatever they did, by Gruumsbaggians who would snatch any piece of paper on which they wrote and tear it into shreds. So no one in Jamesburg was able to complete a false or competing reality successfully. Only under the protection of Ghewen's band was writing possible.

***

Farnstarfl had finally decided that the band of vigilantes could no longer go unopposed. It was unnatural. He had found a videocassette recording of the demonstrators at something called the 1968 Democratic Convention in the city the humans had called Chicago, and it shed some light on the way the humans were supposed to deal with violence. It was fascinating, the way the blue-helmeted men beat the others with their sticks. He decided that would be an excellent model for some opposition to the violent band on Earth. It would help the humans in the violent band to better understand how things actually were in the past and it would help to bring reality one step closer to actual establishment.

There were other things he was working on to help re-establish reality on Earth, too, since he realized humans had entertained themselves before the catastrophe in ways besides books and movies and television and the hokey-pokey.

For example, he was drawing up plans for the reconstruction of what, he learned, had been two of the human race's more

236

important centers for entertainment. One of them had been located, and would be located again, in the place the humans called Florida. It was presided over by an executive who seemed, usually, to dress as a large bipedal mouse, though sometimes he appeared in public as an incoherent duck, or occasionally any one of a number of other animals. The purpose of the place, as far as Farnstarfl could tell, had been to go and wait in very long lines. Farnstarfl was unable to discern exactly what the attraction of waiting in long lines had been to the pre-epidemic humans, but then they had done many other things he still did not completely understand. He was sure, though, that once the place were rebuilt, and the humans were brought there to wait in long lines under the shadows of bizarre-looking struc-tures while the Chief Executive and other officers of the corpora-tion greeted them, they would enjoy themselves, since they had done so in the past.

He could not really understand the other major entertain-ment center he was rebuilding, either. It seemed to have been quite important, especially in New Jersey, and it would not be far from the little human settlement of Jamesburg in which they had made so much progress in restoring the natural order of things. It had been a place where the humans, to amuse themselves, would take money, which they treasured above most other items, to places called casinos, where they would essentially hand it over to the people who ran the facilities. Then the humans, to complete their entertainment, would become aggravated and go home. Again, he didn't quite understand the attraction of this form of entertainment, but he did appreciate that the humans were alien to him and had dif-ferent likes and dislikes. One thing he had concluded, though, was that the humans who ran these casinos did not tell the truth most of the time. He detected a similarity to the cigarette company executives, for he had told the Gruumsbaggian Earth Project workers who were playing the roles of cigarette company executives that they were not to tell the truth at all, ever, about anything.

But he could not spend all his time just with aspects of entertainment. There were so many things to do. His task was so complicated. After tinkering with his plans for a while, he turned his attention to microfilms of some newspapers he had recently received. They were a bit different than the other newspapers he had been working with; they had apparently been found in supermarkets, and they contained some fascinating information. Before he read these newspapers, for example, he had not known human women could sometimes have three-headed lizard babies after the age of sixty, that there had once been herds of featherless, sentient, flesh-eating, seven-foot tall chickens roaming the prairies of North America, or that someone named Ed McMahon had, in fact, been in contact with non-Gruumsbaggian extraterrestrials several times. This last bit was particularly interesting, and Farnstarfl wondered how it could be that the humans, who were restricted mostly to one planet, had encountered other races while the Gruumsbaggians had not.

But that was not a major point. What mattered was that these newspapers, with all their information, would help him refine and improve his restoration of human society. They would help to provide additional guiding principles for the restoration project. It was so complex. He was beginning to feel he needed all the help he could get.

**

238

After The Blue

In the woods where Ghewen and his band had their base, people were mobilizing. Cars were being loaded with hand grenades and rifles and semi-automatics and other weapons. The tanks, which were quite easy to maintain and operate because the Gruumsbaggians had designed them that way, were prepared and arranged in a line. "All right, everyone," Ghewen cried to his assembled band just as they were about to board their vehicles. "You know the direction, and you know what we're doing. Now let's go and show those Gruumsbaggians what's what! On to the Mall of Freehold!"

A cheer erupted from the crowd. Ghewen's charisma and righteous anger had motivated them, and they were ready to go. They roared onto the highway.

The caravan of cars and tanks rumbled rapidly down the highway, ignoring the few remaining strip malls, fast food restaurants, shoe stores, and gas stations, for they had their sights set on bigger prey.

Then they got stuck in traffic. Abruptly the caravan was surrounded by Gruumsbaggians in immobile vehicles, and within a few minutes bored, exasperated human drivers with AK-47s were hanging their hands out the windows, honking at the Gruumsbaggians.

Honking was no use. The Gruumsbaggians did not go any faster. And the humans couldn't blow the Gruumsbaggian vehicles away, because then they would never get to the Mall of Freehold with all the wreckage in the road. It took them three hours to travel the next two miles.

***

Ghewen and his band did not know it, but now their movements were being carefully tracked. Gruumsbaggian monitors were observing every movement with great interest, because Farnstarfl had finally given the order. The band of human vigilantes had done enough for the time being and had to be stopped. Their ultimate destination was continuously being predicted and updated. It was not difficult to do this, since the band was moving at a speed of approximately one and a half miles per hour. The Gruumsbaggians had already identified the Mall of Freehold as a possible target. And if the humans *did* arrive there, they would be greeted by blue-helmeted Gruumsbaggians with truncheons and canisters of tear-gas.

When the Gruumsbaggians decided to end the outbreak of violence, they did not realize that the destruction of Ghewen's band would mean the end of all false realities in and around Jamesburg, but they would have been happy to know it.

***

Jack had not accompanied Ghewen and the rest of the band on this raid. He had discussed this with Ghewen, who agreed that the book was of paramount importance, so Jack stayed at the band's camp in the woods and scribbled furiously away in his haste to complete the book as soon as possible, and, although he did not know it, before it was too late. The writing of the book got easier as he went further and further along. His imagination seemed to grow as he used it. He was driven by his experience in the Gruumsbaggians' office, where he had had to wear outlandish clothes and submit to ridiculous and petty rules and regulations, and where he was monitored by a yellow-skinned, blue-haired creature from outer space. That memory, more than anything, pushed him forward to finish.

He had never wished for anything as he wished for this project to succeed. He wanted desperately to return to his old life, this time with Sheila. He would make it even better because of the limitless possibilities that he now knew reality could hold.

"Are you almost done, Jack?" said Roger Camiglia, Jamesburg's printer. Ghewen had agreed to his staying behind, too, since the Gruumsbaggians couldn't be expected to believe the authenticity of Jack's handwritten manuscript, but they might accept a professional-looking typed microfilm, which Roger could create and age with his equipment. Ghewen had also let Sheila stay behind because he knew her presence was important to Jack, and he knew the importance of the book to all their futures.

"I'll be done in just a few minutes, Rog," Jack said. "I just have a few more paragraphs to write. I hope the Gruumsbaggians aren't too picky about grammar."

"They never taught us much grammar on Gruums-Baag," Sheila said. "It was mostly history and things like that. I don't think they'll be too concerned."

A few minutes later the manuscript was ready. Jack showed it to Roger and Sheila, and after they both skimmed over it they began taking turns typing it out. It wasn't very long, just long enough to convey the necessary information. Roger took the pages and put them through his microfilm-creating equipment. "This rig is one of the latest models from just before the Blue. Still works like a charm," he added. "Rosenthal and the others put it into storage and we didn't need to take it out until fifteen years ago."

When they had produced several microfilms of the book, Jack said, "Now where do we put them? We have to make their discovery look authentic. We can't let what happened last time happen again. This is so important, I don't know how to handle it."

Sheila smiled at him. "I think I know who to give it to. There's a Gruumsbaggian who owes me a favor. His life, I think. He might be convinced to bring it to their attention."

Despite Jack's feelings for her, he had one last pang of doubt about Sheila. He couldn't help wondering if she really wanted the book to succeed. "Sheila," he said, looking imploringly into her eyes, "this is so important to us. I'm still not certain you're sure how you want all this to turn out. You've never lived without Gruumsbaggians. Are you sure you know what you want from all of this?"

"I want what you want," Sheila said simply. Jack smiled as relief swept over him.

***

Fred, the erstwhile manager of the McDonald's that had been Sheila's introduction to the planet of her ancestors, had hung around the rubble of his old restaurant during the few days since its demolition. He had not known what else to do. He had been one of the Gruumsbaggian Empire's legion of unemployed when he was given a wonderful opportunity to work on the Earth Project. But now this place of employment was destroyed. At least his life had been saved by Sheila, his former employee. He had seen how some Gruumsbaggians had been killed by the actions of Ghewen's band. He wondered if this was part of the Earth Project and why management was permitting it—or if things had just gotten out of control.

He had not been given orders about any employment anywhere else, so he had decided the best way to keep his job was to stay at the site and wait for the restaurant to be rebuilt. He felt certain the Earth Project's managers were on top of the situation and would remedy it fairly soon—but he was wrong.

In fact, the regional directors of the Earth Project, the Gruumsbaggians just one or two levels beneath Farnstarfl in the chain of command, had not yet figured out how they were supposed to react to the destruction caused by Ghewen and his band. All they knew was that the destruction was supposed to be allowed to continue. No one had even discussed rebuilding yet.

Fred was sitting on the ground, staring at the pile of rubble, as he had for much of the past three days, when he saw a car drive into the parking lot. He was wondering why any Gruumsbaggians would be bringing their human charges to his restaurant when it was no longer standing, when he saw three full-grown humans emerge from the vehicle. As they came towards him, he felt a shock of recognition. "Sheila!" he said. "You've come back!"

"Hi, Fred! How are you doing? All right, I hope."

"Not too well, Sheila. As you can see, I'm out of a job." Fred felt he could say that, at least, to her. If he'd been a human manager, he would have said that, and he knew his orders for the Earth Project were to pose as human as much as was possible.

"Fred," she said, "I have a favor to ask of you." Fred had finally learned, just a little bit, to recognize human facial expressions and intonations, and he thought he detected something momentous in what she was saying.

"Yes?" he said.

"I know what you and the other Gruumsbaggians are trying to do here on Earth. And Jack and Roger, here, and I and all of the other humans really appreciate it. We know you're sorry about what happened a hundred years ago. But I think the book you'll find on this microfilm," she said, as she handed him a copy, "will be extremely interesting to whoever's in charge. Could you please try to make sure they get it? We think it will have a lot of relevance to the whole project."

"You want me to give it to them?"

Sheila looked at him anxiously. "Fred," she said, "remember the other day, when they blew up the restaurant? They were killing other Gruumsbaggians that day. But I made sure they let you live. Please remember that when you do this one favor. Okay?"

Fred thought for a minute. She had saved his life, and he could find *some* Gruumsbaggian authority to give it to. "Okay," he said. "I'll do it."

"Great! Wonderful! Oh, there's just one more thing. Could you please tell them that you found it somewhere? Don't tell them we gave it to you. That's very important. Okay?"

Fred was confused. That wasn't what had happened! Then he remembered that humans had something called 'lying.' They had discussed it in one of his briefing classes before he came to work on the Project. And his role was to be, as much as possible, like a human McDonald's manager, who, like any human, would have lied sometimes. "Okay," he agreed.

He was just doing his job.

***

After The Blue

After lurching through stop-and-go traffic for four hours, the convoy of tanks and heavily armed cars arrived at the Mall of Freehold. Ghewen leapt out of the lead tank in preparation for one final exhortation to his troops. "All right, everyone!" he yelled. "Now let's show these Gruumsbaggians exactly what we think of them! Let's reduce this so-called Mall to a pile of rubble! By the end of this afternoon I don't want to see a single brick still upright! Are you with me?"

The mixed crowd of refugees from Jamesburg and teenagers who had been taken from the Gruumsbaggian stores and restaurants roared back its approval. "Yes we are!" they shouted, almost in unison.

"Good! Then let's go!"

After they had all synchronized their watches, the crews got back into their tanks and began positioning themselves strategically around the Mall of Freehold. The crews from the cars began assembling their portable rocket launchers and arraying their hand grenades in convenient positions. They hoisted their bazookas onto their shoulders and readied their flamethrowers and then they waited until the pre-arranged time of 1:00 p.m.

The tanks fired first with reverberating booms. Shells hit the sides of the Mall and released cascades of tumbling bricks and showers of crumbling mortar. The walls of the mighty Mall buckled and imploded. The blast from the tanks was followed by a volley of bazooka shots, and then humans holding flamethrowers moved in to finish off anything combustible inside the damaged structure.

A steady stream of Gruumsbaggians dressed in various clerk's uniforms began to issue from the holes in the sides of the building. They ran from the Mall as fast as they could, their long yellow legs making big, loping strides and their four arms furiously flailing. Among them, howling and terribly frightened, was the hippopotamus. It had escaped from its enclosure when a crumbling fragment of the ceiling had landed on the fence, destroying it. The animal ran after the Gruumsbaggians as fast as it could on its short stubby legs.

Ghewen emerged from his tank and waved a fist in the air. "We've got them on the run!" he cried. "It's just a matter of mopping up!" He leapt out of his tank, a semiautomatic clutched in his hands, a bandoleer over his chest, and several hand grenades strapped to his belt. "Follow me!"

Neither he nor his followers saw what was in store for them until it was too late. For on the far side of the Mall an entire battalion of Gruumsbaggians dressed in riot gear had assembled. They wore gas masks and T-shirts emblazoned with the words "Chicago Police," and they carried huge quantities of tear gas and mace. They all carried truncheons. And when they came marching around the mall, tossing cannisters of tear gas everywhere, Ghewen and his band were completely unprepared. The Gruumsbaggians batted a few token swats of their truncheons at some of the tear-gassed humans writhing on the ground and holding their eyes, but not hard enough to actually hurt any of them. "Hippie scum!" some of the Gruumsbaggians yelled as they went about the suppression of the band. Within half an hour it was all over. The humans had all been subdued and were taken to be punished. Then their tarred, feathered, and unconscious figures were deposited near the lake in Jamesburg.

After The Blue

The Mall of Freehold was left a smoldering pile of bricks and mortar, with only a random section of wall still standing. After a few hours, the hippopotamus wandered back and began sniffing and rooting around the rubble. Otherwise, all was calm.

***

Farnstarfl could not believe the wealth, the veritable cornucopia of information he was getting from the microfilms of the tabloid newspapers which he had received. This information was going to be of immense help in furthering the reconstitution of the beauty and intricacy of human society. Before reading it, for example, he hadn't known human women could give birth as early as the age of six or as late as the age of eighty-three, or that some humans could stick their tongues out far enough to lick their foreheads, or that some humans regularly lit their hair on fire as a form of recreation. He decided to begin making plans immediately to incorporate some of these findings into the Earth Project.

Abruptly he was interrupted by one of his aides. "Most high," said the aide, entering his office, "we have just received this new microfilm from Earth. I think you should read it. It is of essential relevance. I am confident nothing we have read previously is as relevant to the Earth Project."

Farnstarfl thanked the aide and accepted the film with great curiosity. He wondered what it was that could be so important. He hoped they offered further refinements, like the new tabloids he had been reading, to what had already been accomplished.

Carefully, he placed the microfilm in the reader. He had become quite proficient at this, and now only got himself tangled in the film once every five or six days. He skimmed over the copy-right pages, which indicated that the book had been written in 1975, decades before the first fatal visit of the Gruumsbaggians to Earth. Quickly, he got to the beginning of the text and started to read.

The very nature of human society has been altered by extraterrestrial beings several times in the past," the book said. "The most recent interference by aliens in Earth's civilization came just two hundred years ago, when the Hespians, who came from a dis-tant galaxy, landed here and tried to promulgate their own version of reality. They felt that it was their responsibility to do this, because they had interfered with the natural development of human society and thrown it off of its natural course. They caused the pyramids and the Sphinx to be built. They also helped to construct the Great Wall of China, and caused their likenesses to be engraved on statues on Easter Island in the Pacific Ocean.

"But the efforts of the Hespians, no matter how successful, would not have brought human society back onto the track it might have followed if left completely alone. For the Hespians were preceded in their interference by other races, such as the Freznaques, the Heptachlors, and the Dibenzofurans. Thus we can only conjecture what human society would have been like today if it had not been for this seemingly interminable series of extraterrestrial interferences. What is clear is that human society, as it is, is far from 'organic;' that is, it is nothing like what it would have been if it had been allowed to develop naturally. We can only hope we have seen the last of the alien interferences in the development of Earth society. But given our history, that is hardly to be expected. And one thing is certain: the present state of affairs is hardly representative of what humans would have constructed in the absence of alien influence. Repeated alien interferences have caused us to live with choking traffic jams, incredible quantities of pollution, and in such a way that we no longer have real communities but only deal with one another in the name of commerce. In doing so, we have been made to live to work rather than working to live, with our lives organized to accommodate work rather than having our work organized to accommodate our lives.

Farnstarfl was as incredulous as it was possible for a Gruumsbaggian to be. He read on and on, about the specific details of each previous alien race's interference in human affairs. And after he had finished, as much as he enjoyed working on the Earth Project, he knew there was only one thing to be done. He was a Gruumsbaggian of integrity, and he was astute enough to realize that the completely natural order of things on Earth could never be restored. It was thousands of years too late for that. He was saddened and disappointed after all the work they had done, but he knew they could not go on. It would be like reconstructing a flaxzen-mour that had already been taken apart and put back together by someone else.

***

One day not long after the Gruumsbaggians had left the planet, Jack, Sheila, Henry, Ghewen, Ghewen's wife, and several others were sitting under the stars on a beautiful, pleasantly cool night in May, sipping their drinks, listening to the chorus of the crickets, and discussing the future. Ghewen and Henry and Jennifer had, of course, been tarred and feathered along with the rest of the band that had assaulted the Mall of Freehold, and while they had experienced some temporary discomfort, the tar had eventually flaked off, and with it the feathers. "It's a good thing we had that little group of vigilantes," Ghewen said to Jack. "Otherwise you never would have had the opportunity to write that book."

"You know, though, a couple of our problems were solved by the Gruumsbaggians' visit," Henry said, and he smiled at the girl next to him. She, like so many other new residents of Jamesburg, had been brought to Earth by the Gruumsbaggians, who had apparently left all of their captive-breeding humans on Earth. The people of Jamesburg could not have been happier. Their problem with genetic diversity had been solved. For the foreseeable future they would not have to regulate marriages.

Ghewen held up a laptop computer he had been fiddling with earlier. "Very true, Henry," he said. "And the electronic equipment and machinery they left here seems to work fine. We won't have to worry about running out of equipment for a long, long time.

After The Blue

If they've left this stuff all over the planet, maybe by the time it does run out, we'll be able to make it again ourselves."

Jack drew Sheila closer to himself. She smiled and rested her head on his shoulder. "But look what they've left us with," he said. "So many of the trees were chopped down. The lake's still not clean. And now there are ruined buildings around here everywhere."

"Wait a minute, Jack," Ghewen said. "Things were like this once before."

"They were? When?"

"You, of all people, should know this. A century ago! Right after the Blue! The Gruumsbaggians were sort of on the mark in some of the things they did. There were riots and panics during the epidemic, so a lot of buildings were damaged in just a few days. But now we have a road system, so we can explore the rest of the continent. And just maybe, they've built functioning airports! Think of the possibilities!"

Jack thought for a moment about the departure of the Gruumsbaggians. The offices and traffic jams and air pollution of the Gruumsbaggians were all gone. The advertisements were starting to wear off most of the animals, and the humans had torn down the billboards. Ghewen was right. In a way, they were in the same position Rosenthal had been after the Blue. They could help to fashion a new world out of the ruins of the old. And they had advantages over those survivors a century earlier. They had Jamesburg, a functioning and intact community, to support them. And they had the legacy of a century of self-sufficiency. Suddenly, Jack was filled with a sense of boundless possibilities. He looked towards the south, down one of the new roads the Gruumsbaggians had left for them, and towards the dark horizon. If he had been able to see far enough, all the way down the empty highway, past the gleaming new rest stops and McDonald's, beyond the new suburban tract houses, he would have glimpsed the half-finished Disney World in Florida, the Chief Executive's uniform hanging by its two ears in a closet.

EPILOGUE

On the planet Thurmiglia, in a galaxy so distant not even the Gruumsbaggians had ever visited it, the inhabitants, who called themselves Thurmiglians, were getting their planet in order. Long ago, they had been one of the most vigorous and adventurous spacefaring races in the entire universe. But then they had fallen upon hard times. They had entered a period of violent civil wars, and their deep-space expeditions all returned home to support their own factions.

Now one side had emerged victorious. This side espoused, among other things, a policy of total non-interference in the affairs of other planets. And it was on record that a Thurmiglian expedition, many thousands of years earlier, had manipulated some quasi-intelligent creatures on the planet Earth through the judicious use of computerized black rectangular slabs. The black slabs, or 'monoliths,' as the Thurmiglians called them, had induced these quasi-intelligent simians to use tools, and fire, and the like. And the present ruling class on Thurmiglia decided that this was wrong, and wanted to make amends.

They knew they never should have interfered, and now they were sending out an expedition to set things right again.

ABOUT THE AUTHOR

Russel Like lives in New Jersey, not far from Jamesburg. He claims that this book is not autobiographical, but the editorial staff at Brunswick Galaxy Press is not so sure.